DANCING ON AIR
BELOW THE SALT SERIES
BOOK FOUR

ELIZABETH ROSE

OLIVERHEBERBOOKS

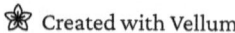 Created with Vellum

NOTE FROM AUTHOR

I wanted to make a note at the beginning of this book regarding the content of this story. While doing research I ran across the fact that back in medieval times, if a noble was to be executed for a crime, he could beg for his life. If it was granted, it was only on the condition that the nobleman agreed to take the place of the executioner from then on. When he someday died as the executioner, his son would be required to follow in his footsteps.

Hence, the nobleman's life was spared, but he and his family would lose their titles, land, money, and most of all, their respect. No one wanted anything to do with executioners or their families. They were avoided like the plague, and treated worse than whores or even lepers.

As soon as I read this, I knew I needed to write a book including a hero who is tortured mentally, being saddled with something like this. What a wonderful challenge!

Without giving away too much of the story, I will say, don't worry if you are squeamish. This is a romance first, and I will only touch on the points of execution and will not be too graphic about it at all. I don't like blood, seeing it in movies, or even reading about it, so you'll never find a lot of gore in my books.

I will say, if a historical romance was really written with the way things were back then, I swear no one would want to read the stories. Or at least, not included in a romance novel, anyway. Torture was common and horrific back in the medieval times. So was the awful way women were treated. Life was hard and conditions were terrible. The streets were filthy, smelly, and disgusting. Personal hygiene wouldn't be at the top of the list either.

Once again, no one wants to read that in a romance novel, so of course, these stories have historical accuracy woven in, but also have a little fantasy mixed in as well so we, as readers, can live through our hero's and heroine's eyes and feel the love without all the negative aspects of the characters' surroundings. I try to keep my books uplifting with empowered heroines (of course), and I like to redeem mentally and physically tortured heroes who might be a little rough around the edges until they meet that perfect woman who helps them meet their true potential of being that knight in shining armor that most women want to see.

I did take the liberty of writing about gallows with a drop-floor in my story. This didn't actually exist yet at this time period. The actual way of hanging a criminal was much more brutal and disgusting. (I won't go into it.) Therefore, this is what I thought would be more palatable for readers.

My story of a hangman is for entertainment purposes only, and for my readers to understand the turmoil my hero is going through. Therefore, I promise to keep things readable so as not to turn anyone away.

Those who have read my books will know that I love to push the envelope, turning and twisting plots and circumstances in ways that might not have been considered by other authors. Here again, I will be doing it once more. (I mean, after all, a noblewoman and a hangman are not a likely pair.)

In my Below the Salt Series, you will find nobles falling in love with commoners. That is something that was forbidden, since nobles needed to marry someone of their same status or possibly even higher. Of course, what fun is that? I like a little more edge and grit to my characters.

Salt was expensive back then, and not for commoners, but nobles had full salt-cellars on their dais tables. They sat on a raised platform to eat, while the servants and commoners sat lower, at trestle tables with benches instead of padded chairs. So, that is where the saying *below the salt* came from. And like I mentioned, nobles were supposed to marry for alliances, titles, and wealth. It would be unheard of, and also forbidden, for nobles to marry anyone from below the salt.

Not in my books, though. (Smile)

So, sit back and relax and read about a man and woman who were originally destined to be together before the unthinkable happens to tear them apart.

Oh, and remember—love conquers all.

Elizabeth Rose

PROLOGUE
ENGLAND, 1369

C onnor Wyland, a lad of sixteen summers, rode through the gates of Marvane Castle in Stockbridge with an entourage of knights and nobles leading the way. After being fostered and trained as a page since the age of seven, Connor had become a squire two years ago. He'd been fostered at Saltwood Castle in Hythe, near the sea. He'd been lucky enough to be personally mentored by the Lord Warden of the Cinque Ports, Garret Blackmore.

Since the age of eight, Connor had been betrothed to the baron's daughter, Lady Eleanor Blackmore. He became best friends with Eleanor through the years, and both of them longed for the day when they would finally be married. Eleanor had been sent to Marvane Castle a few years ago to be fostered by Connor's parents, who lived there under the rule of Lord Clement Sampson, lord of the castle.

Anxious to see Eleanor as well as his family, Connor couldn't wait to get inside. By now, his new sibling should be born. Lord Sampson had planned a festival at the castle, and everyone, including the commoners, were invited to join in the celebration today.

Yes, it was a special day, and the weather was beautiful for this outdoor event. Connor was sure today would be the day when the date of his actual wedding would be chosen and announced as well. After all, things were going smoothly with his training, and his parents were good friends with Eleanor's. The wedding probably wouldn't be for a few years yet, but it felt as if he and Eleanor had always been together.

"Connor," he heard the sweet voice of an angel, turning his head to see the bright red hair of Eleanor as she made her way toward him through the crowd. She was nearly fifteen now, and he couldn't help noticing she had been blossoming into a young lady in his absence. A lady who would one day soon be his wife. This made Connor proud. All he'd ever wanted was to follow in his father's footsteps by having a good wife, a large family, and being an honored knight of the king.

"Eleanor," he called back, with a wave of his hand. Connor jumped off his horse, handing the reins to a stable boy who greeted the traveling party. Although he'd never even kissed his betrothed, he hoped today he'd be able to at least sneak a kiss in the stables with Eleanor before he returned to Saltwood. After all, she would soon be his bride, so what would it matter?

He walked proudly through the crowd, his sword swinging at his side. His training had been going well, and he'd become quite efficient at wielding a blade. The Lord Warden, Eleanor's father, said he would be ready for knighthood well before the required age of twenty-one. This made Connor very happy. Life couldn't get any better. Connor hoped the Lord Warden would somehow make an exception for him and dub him a knight early, before he hit the age of twenty-one. After all, in his opinion, five years was much too long to have to wait. He wanted to be a knight right now.

"Oh, Connor, I'm so sorry." Eleanor pushed her way through the people, throwing herself into his arms.

This was something she had never done before. It surprised and startled him since they had only been friends and never even hugged before now. It was not proper for a lady to act so familiar with a man, especially under the perusal of so many eyes... and wagging tongues. Eleanor had been raised properly and knew what was expected of her. If she was being so careless, it must be because something made her really upset, and Connor needed to find out what that was.

For some reason, the way she was acting sent chills up his spine. Why did he have the feeling that something was terribly wrong? Something that included him? Damn, he didn't want any bad news.

He tried to push that thought from his mind. Connor decided that nothing was going to ruin this happy day for him. His life was going so well and he refused to let anything disrupt it.

"What is it, Eleanor?" he asked, pushing away from her but keeping his hands on her shoulders. It was then that he noticed her light hazel eyes were wet. A tear trailed a jagged path down her cheek. Connor boldly reached out and brushed it away with his thumb, reveling in the softness of her skin beneath his touch. "Why are you crying?" he asked, very confused as to why his betrothed would act this way. Wasn't she as excited to see him as he was to see her? "Has something happened to upset you? I'm here now, Eleanor. You needn't worry. Please don't cry. I will make everything better." Connor tried to act like a man, wanting to protect the girl who would someday be his wife. He had always protected Eleanor, and had even saved her life once as a child. If he hadn't been watching after her, she would have surely drowned that day.

"Connor, it's bad," she said with a sniffle. "So bad that I don't even want to tell you the news."

"It's all right. Be brave," he told her, trying to sound strong like a knight. He tried to act like he knew his father would in times of danger or despair. "You can tell me anything. Whatever it is that is troubling you, we will face it together." His words were meant to calm her, but when he heard her next words, it was he who needed calming instead.

"Y-your mother is dead," she told him, nearly choking on the words.

Her news caught Connor off guard. It caused his blood to freeze in his veins. Then again, it was crowded and noisy in the courtyard with so many nobles and villagers present. He tried to convince himself that he surely must have misheard her. This couldn't be true. Connor had come here today, planning to celebrate the birth of a new sibling. This wasn't at all what he expected. He refused to believe that his mother was gone. This couldn't really have happened.

"What did you say?" he asked, holding his breath, not able to breathe. Mayhap if she said it again, he'd realize she meant something totally different.

"She died, Connor. Your mother is dead," said Eleanor, who had become quite fond of Connor's family. Being fostered by them, she was already like a daughter to his parents, the same way Connor was regarded as a son to her father, Lord Garrett. Eleanor started crying, not able to hold back her emotions anymore.

"Nay. Please tell me it's not true. It can't be." Connor's gaze frantically swept the courtyard, but there were so many people there today that even though he searched for a glimpse of his family, he couldn't find them anywhere.

"It is true," Eleanor continued. "Your mother died two days ago, birthing your baby brother."

"Nay. This can't be," he said, dropping his arms to his sides and shaking his head in denial. He refused to believe that on his happy day he'd hear such horrible news as this. "Where is the rest of my family, Eleanor? Where is my father? Where are my siblings? I need to see them."

"A nursemaid is watching over your newborn brother as well as the rest of your siblings."

"God's eyes, what is going on here? My father should be with them at a time like this. Where in heaven's name is he?"

"Connor," came the shout of his eleven-year-old sister, Francesca, holding the hand of his nine-year-old brother, Leoric, who held on to little Ginevra, who was only four. At the end of the chain of children was the nursemaid, holding a little bundle that he realized was his youngest sibling, his newborn baby brother.

"The baby," muttered Connor, approaching the woman, holding back his tears. He needed to gaze upon his new brother. Surely, this would calm him. Connor respected all life. He felt as if babies were God's gifts to those who pleased him. Connor wanted a large family someday, at least five children like in his family. Mayhap even more. Trying to focus on the miracle of life instead of the grim thought of death, he reached out and moved aside the blanket to see his new brother's face. With a new life, an older one was taken, and this is something he would never be able to accept. His mother was a good, loving woman. She didn't deserve to die. He shook his head sadly. "What is his name?" he asked the nursemaid.

"Your mother named him Alaric right before she died," answered the woman. The baby started to wail. She jostled the infant, trying to quiet him. "The poor little thing must know he's about to lose his father too, with all the crying he's been doing today. What a shame."

Connor's head snapped up. "What did you say?" For the second time that day he found himself praying that he'd misheard someone. Unfortunately, things just kept getting worse.

"Connor, your father is... he is..." started Eleanor, not able to finish her sentence.

"Kill the murderer!" shouted someone from behind him.

The crowd started to push. The people all tried to get to the opposite end of the courtyard for some reason. Connor reached out for his younger siblings so they wouldn't be swept away in the wake. When he looked to where the crowd headed, he spotted something across the courtyard that he hadn't even noticed when he'd arrived. It was the raised platform that was used for executions. He saw a stump at the edge with a basket on the ground below it. A knot twisted in his gut. Why did it look like a beheading was about to happen?

"Bid the devil, what is going on?" asked Connor. "This is supposed to be a festival. Who is being executed today?" He was suddenly afraid he already knew the answer, although it made no sense to him at all.

"It's Father," cried Francesca. "He killed someone, Connor. He's being called a murderer and will die for his crime."

His siblings all started crying at once. The crowd continued to push them along with the swell of visitors over to the executioner's block.

"Wait. Nay. This can't be true." Connor refused to believe it. "Father is a noble. He's a respected knight. He wouldn't kill anyone unless he was attacked first and did it in self-defense."

"Your father was drunk and killed an innocent man," snapped the nursemaid, still trying to calm the baby. "He murdered a noble and now he'll get what he deserves."

6

"Nay! You lie," spat Connor, wanting to strangle the nurse-maid for saying this. He knew his father liked to drink, but this was no reason for the woman to speak badly of him. "My father is a knight and a noble. You are a commoner and should be punished for that remark," snapped Connor. "You don't deserve to watch my siblings. I'll see to it that you are relieved of your position and punished for speaking so brashly."

"Will you, now?" hissed the woman, her eyes turning dark with anger. "Don't bother. I may have been nursemaid to your mother, bless her soul, but she is dead and gone now. I've never cared much for your pompous father, and will gladly leave my position. Since your father is about to be executed anyway, I must point out I have no loyalty to you or your siblings anymore. You will all be orphans now and will have no way to pay me. Well, I don't work for free, I'll have you know. There are other nobles who will pay me well for my services. I'll not be doing charity work with the likes of you and yours. Take the baby. I am tired of his infernal crying. I want nothing more to do with your family." She pushed the baby into Connor's arms, the infant's wailing so loud he could barely think.

"Connor, it's true," said Eleanor, coming to his side. "The nursemaid doesn't lie. Your father was so distraught by the death of your mother that he drank too much in the tavern. And when another noble spoke ill of his dead wife, your father stabbed the man to death in front of everyone. I am told it was a horrific sight."

"God's eyes, nay!" shouted Connor. "I don't believe that Father would do such a thing."

"Out of the way," growled one of the dungeon guards, pushing people aside as he pulled a man along with him who had his hands and feet in shackles and could barely walk without tripping over the heavy chains.

"Father!" shouted Francesca, still crying like the rest of the siblings.

"What? Father?" whispered Connor, his jaw dropping when he turned to see that it was true.

"Children, don't cry," said Connor's father, Sir Wensel Wyland, stopping directly in front of Connor. "Connor, you're here," he said in a soft voice, despair showing in his eyes. "I'm so sorry this happened. Especially on your special day when I was going to announce when you'd actually be married to Eleanor. You are doing so well with your training too. You do not deserve this."

"Father, you're a noble. They can't kill you," shouted Connor, grasping for a stich of hope, but coming up empty.

"Aye, sadly they can, Son," said Wensel, his gaze dropping to the ground. "I was careless and let my anger control my actions. I killed a noble, it is true. Now, I will die because of it. I am so sorry, Connor. I was upset about losing Mary," he said, speaking of his departed wife. "She fought so hard to live, but birthing the baby was too much of a toll on her body. Son, you are the eldest and in charge of the family now."

"Nay. Don't say that." Connor shook his head furiously, as if by doing this he could rid himself of this horrible nightmare that was unfolding right before his eyes. "I'm going to become a knight someday, just like you. I will do it, and you will be here to see it happen. It's true. You'll see."

"I believe you. But I won't be here to see it, I'm sorry." The chains attached to the shackles around his wrists rattled as he lifted his hands but couldn't reach Connor. "I am proud of you, and wish things were different right now. Sadly, it is my time to leave this world forever. Take good care of your siblings," said Wensel. "Do it for your mother."

"Nay! They can't kill you, Father. I won't let them."

"Come on, you bloody cur," snapped the guard, giving the chains a yank. It jerked his father forward and he fell to the ground. Connor realized his father had been beaten in the dungeon. His clothes were torn and bloodied and he looked gaunt and pale.

"Eleanor, take the baby," said Connor, pushing the newborn into the girl's arms. "I have to help my father."

Connor lifted his father to his feet, feeling the man's body shaking under his grasp. Even the bravest of knights wasn't impervious to the executioner's blade. Connor couldn't even imagine what his father was feeling right now. The guard pulled him away.

"Papa," yelled Francesca, starting to run after him, but Connor reached out and grabbed her by the arm to stop her.

"Hold tightly to Leoric and Ginevra," he told his sister. "Stay by Eleanor. Eleanor, please take them away from here so they don't have to watch this."

"Come with me," said Eleanor, holding the baby and reaching out for the other children with her free hand. "We'll wait in the stable for Connor to return."

"Connor," said his father, looking back over his shoulder into Connor's eyes. Reflecting back at Connor was fear and despair and total devastation. "There is nothing you can do to save me. Please promise me you'll take good care of your siblings, that's all I ask."

"You know I will," said Connor, struggling to hold back the tears as he followed on his father's heels. Out of the corners of his eyes he saw the executioner climbing the platform with his huge, sharp sword in his hand. The messenger of death wore a long, black cloak with a hood covering his head.

"Don't leave us, Father," begged Connor, even though he knew it made no difference what he said. There was nothing anyone could do to stop the horrific action that was about to take place. "First Mother, and now you? We'll be orphans."

His father stopped in his tracks. "Nay, I don't want my children to end up as orphans." Then he was yanked away once again and had to take small, quick steps since the shackles and chains that bound him kept him from any big movements. He looked over his shoulder at Connor and it was then that Connor accepted the fact his father would be beheaded right in front of him. The thought terrified him and he found himself not even able to move. He prayed to God to save his father. He wished for a way to stop this from ever happening.

The crowd cheered and shouted, and some even threw rotten fruit at Connor's father as he passed by. These bloodthirsty fools wanted a beheading. They all fought for a spot in the front so they wouldn't miss every gory detail. What was wrong with them? Why should anyone want to see a single person die? Connor could never get used to this, and neither would he ever understand this as long as he lived. Life was to be celebrated, but not someone's death.

The dungeon guard hauled Connor's father up to the top of the platform where the executioner awaited them. He used a stone to sharpen his massive sword that would be used for the beheading. This was the weapon used by executioners in instances such as this.

"Nay," mumbled Connor, as the guard pushed his father to his knees, fastening a bag over his head. He then held his head down atop the stump. A basket was strategically placed on the ground in front of the platform to aid in the decapitation.

Connor felt as if he were going to retch. The shouts from the crowd got louder. Many of the men raised tankards of ale to their mouths, and others were even laughing. To them, this was naught but a form of entertainment.

"Nay. This is wrong," mumbled Connor, not willing to

stand here and watch as his father's life was ended. Connor needed to at least try to do something to save him, even if his efforts were not fruitful.

Running to the platform, he pushed several people aside and climbed the stairs, only stopping when he came toe-to-toe with the feared hangman—or executioner, as the man was called by both titles.

"Don't hurt my father," shouted Connor with his hand on the hilt of his own sword. He supposed his action was taken as a threat because a guard ran up the stairs after him, taking away his sword and throwing it down. He gripped Connor tightly by the shoulder.

"Go home, boy," said the executioner, lifting his sword to show that he meant what he said. The sun made a glare from the shiny metal, hitting Connor directly in the eyes. "There is nothing you can do to stop this. You don't want to watch it, I assure you. It won't be pretty."

"But that's my father!" exclaimed Connor, seeing the first guard holding his father in the kneeling position with his foot against his back now.

"Go to your mother, boy, where you belong," snarled the guard in a gruff voice. He still held on to Connor although Connor struggled against him to try to help his father.

"My mother is dead," said Connor. "And stop calling me boy! I swear to God I will not let you take my father's life." He tried to reach for his sword, but the guard pulled him over to the steps of the platform.

"Kill him! Kill him!" chanted the crowd, growing into a frenzy. Connor looked down at the faces of the people, hating each one of them right now for wanting to see his father beheaded. Some of the women even brought along their children and baskets of food. It all made him want to retch.

"Get him off the platform," yelled a man, swishing his

hand through the air. When Connor looked closer, he realized the man speaking was Lord Sampson. He was lord of Marvane Castle, and also the one who commanded the executions of the prisoners. "Remove him and continue with the execution."

"What? Nay, please, Lord Sampson," begged Connor. "You cannot kill my father. He hasn't even had a trial. This isn't fair."

"Fair?" asked Sampson. "Your father killed my brother, and for that he has been condemned to death. He killed a noble and no trial is needed. He will die for his crime, and it will happen today with everyone watching."

"I'm sure it's all a misunderstanding," yelled Connor.

"The only misunderstanding is your foolish notion that you can stop this, boy. Guard, get the fool off the platform before I have to come up there and do it myself."

"Don't call me *boy*," shouted Connor, hating how everyone seemed to dismiss him because they didn't think his opinion was important.

"Come, boy. You're about to become a man when you witness what is about to happen," laughed the dungeon guard, kicking Connor's sword down the stairs.

"Nay," spat Connor. "I'll be a knight someday, just like my father."

The guard laughed, hauling Connor to the stairs now. "You had better hope you're nothing like your bloody father. Unless you want to be beheaded as well."

He pushed Connor and sent him tumbling down the stairs, head over heels. Connor landed on his back on the ground next to his sword. So many angry faces stared down at him. He swore he could feel their hatred, yet they had no real reason to want his father dead since it didn't involve them. Connor could barely breathe from the force of the fall and was surprised he hadn't broken his neck.

"Move out of the way! Let me through." Eleanor pushed

people aside and fell to her knees next to him. "Connor, are you all right?" Her bright red hair had become loose and blew past her face in the breeze. Her eyes that held all the concern in the world stared directly at him. He felt as if she could see down to his very soul.

"Eleanor?" He pushed up to a sitting position, feeling achy and dizzy. "I told you to stay with my brothers and sisters and to keep them away from here." He reached out and rubbed his throbbing arm.

"They are in the stable and are fine; don't worry. Connor, I want to remind you that my father is here. He will help you. I am sure he will do something, since he is friends with your father."

Connor got to his feet to see Lord Warden Garrett Blackmore, Eleanor's father and also his mentor, making his way over to Lord Sampson.

"What is going on, here?" growled Garrett.

"This man killed my brother," snapped Sampson.

"Sir Wensel is a noble and an honored knight," Garrett told him. "Why is he on the executioner's block?"

"He's a noble and a knight, that's right," said Sampson. "He also killed another noble, and because of it, he will die," snapped Sampson. "It's the law."

"Take that bag off the man's head at once," ordered Garrett, looking up to the top of the platform.

"Blackmore, this is my castle, and even you can't stop the execution of this man," Sampson warned him. "I don't care if he is your friend, it no longer matters."

"I am a Lord Warden and will have the final say. Has he had his last words yet?" asked Garrett.

"Nay," said Sampson. "But what does it matter? He is a drunk and has nothing worth listening to anyway."

"Executioner, put down your blade and let the man speak,"

commanded Garrett in a loud voice. "Quiet. Everyone quiet!" shouted Garrett with his hand above his head. Finally, the crowd settled down.

"My lord?" asked the executioner in confusion, looking down at the men.

"Fine. Let the condemned have his last words," said Sampson with a shrug as if he thought this was all a waste of time.

The executioner lowered his sharpened blade to his side while the guard pulled the hood off of Connor's father's head.

Connor walked over with Eleanor and stood next to her father, waiting to hear what his own father's last words would be.

"Do you have anything to say, you fool?" ground out the prison guard. "If so, speak now."

"Any final request?" asked the hangman. When he tilted his head upward, the sun hit his face. Connor cringed on seeing the burn mark across the executioner's cheek, a sign of the many lives he'd taken, and a warning mark for everyone to stay away. He was old with gray hair and had many wrinkles on his weathered face. That made Connor wonder if this was the only profession the man had ever known. Sad to think that anyone would have such a job. No one ever spoke to execution-ers, and they were treated worse than if they had the plague. It was not a desirable job at all. It made Connor wonder why anyone would ever want to do it.

"Is there any way you can help me, Lord Warden? Please." Connor's father begged for assistance, but by now anyone could see that there was nothing that could be done. His father had made a bad choice. He'd made a horrible mistake, and now he would die for his actions.

"The law states that anyone killing a noble must die,"

Garrett reminded him. "Was it done in self-defense, Sir Wensel?"

Connor's eyes locked with his father's. "Say yes, say yes," whispered Connor, hoping if his father said this, his life might be spared.

"Nay. It wasn't," growled Sampson. "And I have a dozen witnesses who will testify that this man stabbed my brother to death as they drank. Sir Wensel killed an unarmed man."

"Unarmed? Is this true?" Garrett asked Connor's father. "Did you kill a man who had no means of protecting himself?"

Connor's heart stood still and he held his breath, waiting for his father's answer. What the man said right now would determine his fate.

"I was drunk, Garrett," spat Wensel. "Mary died birthing our baby. Sampson's brother insulted my dead wife and it made me angry."

"But my brother was unarmed! Tell everyone the truth, or do I need to call upon my witnesses?" asked Sampson. "We can have a trial right here if need be."

"Nay. Don't admit it, Father." Connor shook his head, but his father looked away and answered.

"It is true," he answered, so softly that people in the crowd started shouting for him to speak louder.

"I can't hear him," called out a man in the back.

"Speak up, you fool," said a fat, ugly, old woman.

"Say it loud enough so that everyone can hear you, murderer," snarled Sampson.

"It is true! I murdered an unarmed noble," yelled Wensel, sealing his doomed fate.

"Nay, Father. Why did you say that?" whispered Connor, closing his eyes, feeling as if he were about to cry, but trying to stay strong in this wretched time of turmoil.

"Father, do something to help him," begged Eleanor, tugging at the Lord Warden's sleeve.

"I'm sorry, Eleanor, but it is the law. There is no way for him to escape his death now," answered Garrett. "Well, just one way, actually, but it isn't something that any noble would ever consider."

"What? What is it?" asked Connor anxiously, hoping for anything to redeem his father and save the man's life. "Tell me. Save my father, please."

"Continue with the execution," shouted Sampson, causing the executioner to raise his sword once more and step closer to the condemned man.

"Father, tell him," Eleanor cried. "Hurry. Whatever it is, let it be Sir Wensel's decision if he'll agree to it or not."

"Wait!" called out Garrett, stopping the executioner once again.

"Dammit, stop stalling," Sampson ground out. "There is no way this man can escape his death and you know it. He will die for what he did."

"There is one way he can be spared; however it would have to be up to Sir Wensel if he agrees to the decision or not," said Garrett loud enough for everyone to hear.

The crowd spoke softly to each other, not understanding what was going on. Neither did Connor.

"Well, what is it?" asked the guard.

"The law states that a condemned noble can only escape his death if he assumes the position of hangman," said Garrett.

"What?" asked Connor. "Nay," he said, shaking his head. "No one wants to be the hangman. My father is a respected knight."

"Not anymore, he isn't," said one of the prison guards with a chuckle.

"Really? My life will be spared if I take over the executioner's job?" Connor's father looked over at them once again.

"Yes. That is, if the executioner agrees to giving up his position," said Garrett. "Executioner, what do you say?"

The executioner slowly lowered his sword as well as his hood. "I—I don't know what to say. I have been the executioner ever since I inherited the job from my deceased father many years ago," said the man of death. "It is all I've ever known my entire life. My father was the town's butcher at one time, until he was forced to take the job because a hangman was needed."

"So, what are you saying?" snapped Sampson. "Do you want to keep the job you have or give it up?"

"I would love to live out the rest of my life not being burdened with this awful position again," said the executioner. Connor swore he saw the man quickly brush a tear away, which surprised him since he didn't think anything could ever upset a hangman.

"I see. What about you, Sir Wensel? Do you agree to this ridiculous trade?" asked Sampson.

"Wait." Garrett raised a hand in the air. "Before you answer, Sir Wensel, you must know something. In sparing your life, you will also be condemning the lives of your entire family. You will be forced to give up your title, holdings, money, and all respect. And when you die, your son will need to take your place as the hangman."

"What?" Connor's head snapped around. "I don't want to ever be a hangman. I'm going to be a knight. You know that, Lord Warden."

"Father, what will this mean for Connor and me if his father agrees to the trade?" Eleanor asked Garrett. "Remember, we're betrothed."

"I'm sorry, Daughter, but if Connor's father agrees to take

the position of the executioner, you'll never be able to see or be with Connor again. The betrothal will be nullified."

"Nay!" cried Eleanor. "I want to marry Connor. It is what we've planned for so long. I want to be his wife someday. I could never stop seeing him. He is my best friend."

"This is crazy," Connor complained, not wanting his father to die, but also not wanting to lose Eleanor. It was also horrifying to think his family would lose their titles, holdings, and all respect. Plus, not to mention, any chance of ever being a knight would be gone.

"I—I don't know what to do," said his father, his eyes once again settling on Connor. Connor stood frozen, not knowing what to say or how to respond.

"Father, don't die!" Just then, Connor's siblings rushed through the crowd, crying and staring up at their father with wide eyes. It about broke Connor's heart.

"Children," said Wensel, still in a kneeling position with his hands bound behind him. "Please, leave. I don't want any of you to watch me die."

"So, you are choosing to die then?" asked Sampson impatiently. "Make your decision. We are waiting."

"Connor? Son, tell me what to do," said Wensel, looking to Connor for his answer. Connor saw his father's body shaking. This unnerved Connor. His father had always been a strong and confident man until today. He had been the backbone of their family. Now, he shook with fright, not even able to make the decision of what would happen to him and his family. Worst of all, he was asking Connor to make that decision for him.

"Father," wailed little nine-year-old Leoric. "I'll save you." He rushed for the stairs of the platform, but Connor reached out and grabbed his little brother by the arm and held him tightly.

Connor looked over to his sister Francesca, rocking their crying newborn brother Alaric in her arms. The little boy would never have the chance of knowing either of his parents if his father died. That hardly seemed fair. And what would the rest of his sisters and brothers do, being orphans? Connor couldn't bear to see his siblings split up and placed in the homes of different families to be raised. They wouldn't even have the luxury of growing up in a castle, as they'd be shunned by the nobles since their father was convicted of murdering a nobleman. Nobody would even want them. Or at least he didn't think so. Francesca looked over at Connor with tears in her eyes, waiting for him to answer.

"Tell Father to take the trade," begged Francesca. "Connor, we just lost Mother and cannot lose Father too. We need a father. We can't survive on our own."

Leoric struggled against Connor's hold. His four-year-old sister Ginevra rushed over to him and fell to the ground crying, clinging to Connor's leg. This was all too much. This was supposed to have been a happy day. Connor had been looking forward to coming to the festival and possibly even kissing Eleanor for the first time. How had things gone wrong so quickly?

"Eleanor," said Connor, looking over at his betrothed. She stared at him with those big hazel eyes filled with tears, waiting for him to decide his father's fate, just like everyone else. Bid the devil, why did he have to be the one put in this position?

Time stood still and every second seemed like an hour to Connor. Why the hell was his father asking him what he should do? If he told his father not to accept the deal, the man would be beheaded in front of all his children. It would be devastating! No child should have to see that. It would also scar his siblings for life.

19

If his father's life was spared, Connor's dream of someday becoming a knight would be shattered. He would be labeled an outcast from this day forward. The only profession he'd ever know would be as hangman when his father passed on. All Connor wanted right now was to turn back time so he could have somehow kept his father from killing anyone.

He looked over at Eleanor again, and she seemed terrified. She wiped a tear from her eye. This wasn't getting any easier.

His siblings wailed. They needed a father. But did anyone really need a father who was a hangman? If Connor's father's life was spared, it would condemn his entire family to hell, because that is what their lives would be from now on.

"Son? It is up to you," said his father. "Do I die? Or do I live?"

"Damn you," Connor ground out under his breath. He shouldn't be the one making this decision. He was only sixteen years old. He now regretted even being here today at all.

"Connor, don't let father die," wailed Leoric. "Save him."

"We just lost Mother. We can't lose him too," said Francesca once again. "Please, Connor. Don't let him die."

"Well? Answer your father, boy," snapped the impatient Lord Sampson.

"Father," said Connor, feeling as if he were the one about to be condemned to death right now. He'd be damned with either decision, and was sure to regret it for the rest of his life. He looked back at Eleanor once more, his heart feeling so heavy in his chest. "I'm sorry, Eleanor," he whispered. "I just can't let him die."

"Connor, please! I don't want to lose you," begged Eleanor, crying even harder.

Connor slowly turned back to face his father. "Your family... needs... you," said Connor, holding one arm around his brother and the other around his sister. He looked back to see

Eleanor holding her hand over her mouth. She spun around on her heel and fled through the crowd.

Connor had given the only answer he could. He had pushed all his dreams aside, because even if his father had made a horrible mistake, the man didn't deserve to die because of it. It had been done in grief over losing his wife. He had been protecting his loved one like he always did—even if the woman was dead. Connor's heart ached for his mother and he understood how badly his father must be missing her as well. The loss of a loved one can make anyone do things they normally wouldn't. After just losing his mother, Connor didn't want to lose his father as well. This was too much agony for one day.

"Yes?" asked Connor's father, his voice shaky. "I should accept the deal?" he asked Connor, double-checking.

Connor's jaw was clamped too tightly to even speak. All he could do was to give a small nod.

"Then I accept the position of hangman," said Connor's father, getting boos and more shouts and swearing from the crowd. "I accept the trade in exchange for my life."

"The decision has been made. Get those chains off of him," shouted Garrett. "Let the man off the platform anon."

"Executioner, hand over your sword and robe to the fool who will now take your place." Sampson had the nerve to actually chuckle. "Wyland, take your cursed family out of here and wait to be called upon for your first job."

"Thank you. Thank you, my lords." Wensel stood up and rubbed his wrists after the guard had removed his shackles.

"Oh, just one more thing," said Sampson, sounding like he was enjoying all this. "The new hangman will need to be marked so no one mistakes him as a noble. Ever."

"Sampson, let it go," muttered Garrett, but the evil man wouldn't let up.

"Blacksmith," called out Sampson. "Bring me a hot poker from the forge immediately."

"Wait. What are you doing?" asked Connor, his stomach feeling like it was about to turn inside out.

"It's all part of the new job," said Sampson. "Guard, bring the new hangman to me anon."

Connor held tightly to his crying siblings as the guard hauled his father down to Lord Sampson.

"Here you are, my lord," said the blacksmith, as he returned with the glowing poker in his hand. "It is red hot, so be careful." Lord Sampson took the cool end of the poker.

"No one will mistake you for who and what you really are now, you murderous bastard!" Sampson reached out with the hot poker, drawing it slowly across Wensel's cheek. Wensel cried out and backed away, leaning over to hold his marred face. The stench of burnt flesh filled the air.

"Nay! You cur! You can't do that." Connor dropped the hands of his siblings and approached Lord Sampson. "You just wanted to hurt him for killing your brother—admit it."

"Connor, step back," warned Garrett, but Connor was too angry to listen.

"You are the hangman's son and when he dies, you'll take his place," said Sampson. "I think it's only right that you be marked as well."

Before Connor even realized what the man said, he felt the end of the hot poker against his own cheek. Searing pain flowed through him, causing him to cry out in pain. He felt the hands of the Lord Warden on his shoulders, pulling him away.

"Drop the damned poker and leave this family alone, Sampson," commanded Garrett. "You have already caused them enough trouble and had no right to mark the boy, too."

"Get them out of here," ordered Sampson. "I want the bastard and his family off my lands immediately. Everyone, get back to work and to your homes. The festival is cancelled. Go now. No more gawking here. The day is done." Sampson threw the hot poker to the ground and left, being followed by the reluctant crowd, still sore that they came for a festival, were promised a killing, and they didn't get either one.

"Are you all right?" Garrett asked Connor.

Holding his burned cheek, Connor looked up to the scar on the Lord Warden's face that started under his left ear and followed his jawline. He'd always had it as far as Connor knew, but Connor had thought it was just a wound from war. Now, he wasn't so sure.

"The burn hurts, but I'm fine," said Connor. "Lord Warden, were you a hangman once, too? I see you also have a scar on your face."

"Nay, I wasn't, Connor. My scar is a wound I received saving another's life. But that is not important now," said Garrett. "Connor, I'm sorry, but I have to tell you that you will not be marrying my daughter anymore."

"I... I know," he said, looking around for Eleanor, but she was nowhere to be found.

"Where will my family live now?" asked Connor's father, as his children all ran to him and hugged him in relief.

"Not at the castle, that's for sure," said Garrett. "You'll have to find a cottage of wattle and daub outside of town, since the townsfolk won't accept you either. I'm sorry. You are free to go now."

"Thank you, for your help, my lord," said Wensel, holding back his tears by biting his lip. "I just couldn't bear the thought of never seeing my children again." He took the newborn baby from Francesca and cradled it gently against his chest. The baby finally stopped crying.

"I understand your decision, but I will miss the fact that our children were supposed to be wed," said Garrett. He looked at Connor and shook his head in pity. "This boy was destined to become a knight, and from what I've seen he would have made a damned fine one, too. But now, I am sad to have to say that Connor will never be anything... other than a hangman's son."

CHAPTER I
FIVE YEARS LATER

T he most despised man in all of England was none other than the hangman.

Connor Wyland's father had sold his soul to the devil five years earlier when he agreed to take the position of the hangman in order to save his life. By doing so, Connor's family was also shunned and hated. It was a decision to save one man's life, and ruin so many others in return.

Once being a noble and highly respected, Connor had hoped to follow in his father's footsteps to become a knight someday. He most likely would be knighted by now if things hadn't changed so fast and drastically. Now, instead of ever having the chance to become a knight, the only thing Connor's future held was disgust, guilt, loneliness, isolation, and deep remorse. The only promise in Connor's future was the one of someday burning in hell for all eternity.

For the past five years he had assisted his father in taking the lives of the condemned. Connor felt condemned as well. He would follow in his father's footsteps, just like he'd always aspired to do, but unfortunately this wasn't the profession he ever hoped to hold.

Connor waited now at his father's side atop the gallows, ready to assist him with the hanging. His only reason for even being here was that his father insisted he learn the trade—if killing people was really even considered a trade. Connor wasn't even sure. Lately, his father had been sickly, and it seemed as if he became weaker every day. Learning to take a prisoner's life was the last thing in the world Connor ever wanted to do. He respected life of all kinds. Death—or causing a death—was against everything he'd ever believed in.

Connor learned to become calloused over the years, having had to tamp down his feelings when he walked down a road and people ran the other way or talked about him behind his back. His family hadn't even been able to live in town because no one wanted them anywhere near them. A hangman and his family were considered trash. They were considered despicable by most people, and often were spit upon as they walked past. There was no way Connor would want to live in town with those who hated him now. Instead, he and his family lived in a hut made of wattle and daub deep in the forest, with no protection from the knights of the castle at all.

Connor was in training to someday take his father's place, since there was no other job for him to pursue. Of course, there wasn't a man to execute every day, so to earn extra money to live on, he had to clean out gong pits, shoveling up feces from castles and monasteries. Another job was collecting taxes from whores, and on occasion even working at the tanning pits. These were jobs that no one wanted to do. The cesspools and the tanning pits smelled so foul that they caused people to vomit just being near them.

Connor lived in hell now, and nothing was ever going to quench the fires that threatened to burn his soul. This was a life that could never be changed. And it was also a decision that Connor wished he had never had to make.

Ignored, but not forgotten, Connor's emotions always caused a knot to form in his stomach at every execution he attended. Even though Connor wasn't yet the one pulling the lever or swinging the blade, he knew someday he'd have to carry on in his father's wake. His job now was to learn the ropes, so to speak, by helping his father cut down the bodies from the nooses afterwards. He also collected body parts and made sure all the corpses were buried after the executions. However, Connor refused to be the actual one who took the life of a defenseless person, no matter how guilty they were or what kind of crime they'd committed.

Some nobles liked to display the dead in gibbets, or hanging cages afterwards. It was supposed to scare others from committing the same crimes. Connor always made sure to pay the lords from his own pocket to let him bury those bodies right away. He saw no need for this sort of torture to the loved ones of those slain.

This damned job never got any easier, and only promised to get worse with each passing day. His father had been pestering him to make the final blow of a blade or pull the damned lever of the gallows himself by now. Still, he hadn't. Connor had fought his father, not wanting to do it now or ever.

The condemned man today was a mere thief here at Marvane Castle—the place his family hated more than anywhere else. The thief was young, and his family watched from the front row. The condemned man's wife held her crying children to her bosom.

God's eyes, Connor's heart went out to them. He hated executions, and especially ones that took place here. It felt like Lord Sampson purposely condemned more men than other lords did, and sentenced them to die. It was obvious that he

27

wanted Connor and his father to continue to be tortured for the death of the man's brother. Would this ever end?

Watching the wife and children of the thief, it felt no different to Connor than when he and his siblings watched as his father was almost beheaded. It was the hardest thing in the world to face... or was it? Connor felt as if being in this position was all his fault since he'd told his father to do whatever it took to save his life.

If Connor had realized five years ago just how awful this life was going to be, mayhap he would have watched his father die that day after all. Instead, his whole family had been cursed and suffered every day because of his father taking the deal of being the hangman in return for his life being spared.

Had Wensel Wyland been killed that day, it would have been horrific and hard to forget. But at least Connor wouldn't have to keep reliving that incident day after day, watching others in the same position as his family and father once were.

Damn it—why had his father even asked him to make the decision that day? Why the hell did Connor, at only sixteen years of age, have to decide a man's fate? It wasn't his decision to make, and he never should have done it.

Connor told his father to save his own life that day, only thinking of his young siblings and the fact they'd just lost their mother and needed a father in their lives. Plus, Connor loved his father and didn't want the man to die, of course. Then again, even as horrible as that would have been, at least Connor wouldn't have been the one to condemn his family. He also wouldn't have to be a major part of watching so many others go to their deaths... and feeling like each one was somehow all his fault, as well.

One life saved five years ago, but so many others taken since then.

Had it really been a fair trade after all?

Had Connor made a wrong decision that day, and doomed his entire family for life because of not being able to let go?

"Forgive me," Connor's father whispered into the ear of the condemned man, placing the noose around the thief's neck.

The hangman asking the man who was about to die for forgiveness was normal. After all, a hangman was only doing his job. Most of the condemned realized taking a life wasn't what an executioner or anyone really wanted to do.

"Y-you're forgiven, hangman. Take my coin. Please." The prisoner looked back over his shoulder at Connor's father, giving him the coin clutched tightly in his bound hands behind his back. Fear filled the thief's eyes. "Now, you will assure me this will be a clean and fast death, and that my soul will get to heaven?"

"Don't worry, you won't suffer. I'll make certain it is a clean and fast break. However, where your soul goes afterwards is not up to me," mumbled Connor's father, taking the coin and tossing it over to Connor. Connor caught it in one hand, swearing he could feel the blood money burning into his palm the same way that hot poker had scorched his face five years ago. His scar throbbed. He brushed his hand over it, willing it to disappear, but knew it wouldn't. He was scarred for life in more ways than one. The sadness inside him hardened his heart and made him angry at everyone—especially himself. Connor hated himself for his decision and for whom he had become. He was actually no longer sure he could love anyone in this lifetime. He didn't deserve happiness. And as much as he missed Eleanor, he hoped she had found a nobleman to marry and had moved on with her life.

"I only stole to feed my family," wailed the man. "Please, don't kill me for wanting to provide for my hungry wife and children."

Connor's father ignored him and continued to place a black

hood over the man's head. Wensel Wyland never showed any emotion when killing a man. Connor supposed it was because he was once a knight of the king, and had gone to war and killed many on the battlefield. The only time Connor saw his father break down was at the death of his wife. Connor's parents had been in love from the day they'd married. Love in a noble marriage usually didn't exist, since weddings took place for the purposes of alliances only. His parents were lucky to have found love. Connor was sure he could have found love with Eleanor, too. But that was before. Now, things were different and love no longer mattered or existed for him.

He pocketed the coin, feeling disgust at all of this. After what Connor had been through in his life, he no longer believed in heaven. To him, hell surely existed though. Hell was where he lived every day of his life.

He looked down at the crowd of people watching the execution. Most of them were drinking and laughing, since executions were naught but entertainment for them. The rich took their positions near the front of the gallows, not wanting to miss a thing.

The thief's wife continued to cry and hold her children tightly. Then a group of nuns hurried in and knelt down right in front, starting to pray.

Dammit, he hated when they did this. Why couldn't they stay at the abbey or in church where they belonged? This only made matters harder for Connor. He saw a cloaked woman with the nuns today. She rushed over to the soon-to-be widow and her children and wrapped her arms around them in a hug, trying to comfort them. Then that same woman turned to look up at him. When she did, her hood was blown off her head from the wind.

Connor froze. His eyes opened wide and he forced himself to take a step to the edge of the gallows to get a better look at her. He wasn't sure at first, since it had been so long. But then his heart almost stopped in his chest, and he realized just whom he was looking at.

"Eleanor," he whispered, seeing his betrothed comforting the family of the condemned man. Connor hadn't even seen Eleanor since that horrible day when his future changed forever. She seemed to have disappeared, and actually, it made things a little easier, not having to confront her. She was a girl then, but now—now she was a beautiful woman.

Long, curly red locks of hair fell around her shoulders, seeming to bounce every time she moved. Her body had filled out with delectable curves. She was dressed in the fine clothes of a noble under her cloak. God's teeth, she was a sight for sore eyes.

"Connor. Son," said his father, coughing, his chest rattling loudly. "It's time. You pull the lever today. You need to start doing it."

"What?" Conner whirled around to face his father. He was only there to assist. Not to do anything other than to collect the dead body and haul it away. Or so he'd told himself, since that was the only thought that helped ease his pain and discomfort. "Nay, I don't think so."

"You are twenty-one now, and have been in training for this for the last five years. It is time for you to start taking control of the executions. Soon, this job will be yours, and I need to know that you can do it."

"Nay, I can't do it, and neither do I want to be the one doing the execution."

"You have to, Connor. You don't have a choice." He coughed again.

"Well, I don't want to take a life. I didn't choose this profession—you did." Anger welled within him, more so at

31

himself than his father right now for ever letting things get so out of hand.

"Nay, you chose it for me, in case you've forgotten. You chose this life for all of us, Connor."

"Dammit, stop saying that!" Connor felt ready to explode with anger.

"If you didn't want to become the hangman someday, then you should have just let me die," continued his father. "Are you regretting your decision?" His father's sorrowful eyes bore into him, making Connor realize how insensitive he was being about this harrowing situation.

"Nay. Of course not. I'm sorry," whispered Connor. "Of course, I didn't want you to die. But you never should have expected me to make that decision in the first place. It wasn't right and you know it."

"Bid the devil, Connor, stop wallowing in guilt and step up and be a man! If you were a knight right now, you would have gone to battle and killed many men already. This is no different."

"It is different," Connor told him. "First of all, I am not a knight, although it was all I ever dreamed of being. And second, if I were a knight, I would have killed armed men. In battle. In self-defense," Connor corrected him. "Men who were able to fight for their lives." His gaze shot back to the condemned man. "Not a man tied up and vulnerable, just waiting to be killed."

"You sound as if you think we're killing innocent people," snapped his father. "This man is a prisoner and deserves to die."

"Really. Just like you deserved it?" he asked, seeing the pain in his father's eyes when he said it.

"As much as it hurts to hear you say that, I know it is true, Son. I did deserve to die," his father choked on the words. "I killed a man. By rights, I should be dead right now. Why didn't you tell me to accept the blade to my neck? Why couldn't you talk me out of taking this trade instead of accepting the fate I truly deserved?"

"Oh, no you don't! Don't lay this on my shoulders and make this *my* mistake," growled Connor. "If you had been a man, just as you are now accusing me of not being, you would have taken what you deserved and not asked a mere boy to make your decision for you."

"I was confused. I was about to die, for God's sake. Anyone in my position would have panicked and done the same. I knew I couldn't think straight at that moment, and had relied on you to do it for me."

"Well, you could have rejected my decision."

"I could have, that's true. But I only did it for you and my other children." They stared at each other and the air became thick between them. Finally, his father looked down and shook his head in shame. "I know now that it was a mistake, and for that, I am sorry."

Now Connor felt even worse. "You're not dead yet," he told his father. "This job is your profession right now, not mine." Connor reminded him. "And until you do die, I'm not going to do your bidding for you. This is all on your head for now."

"I'm sick and dying, in case you haven't noticed. You need to learn the profession. This job will be yours soon, and you will have no choice but to take it."

Conner's gaze flashed back to the ground where he saw Eleanor watching him intently with those big, beautiful hazel eyes, that were so light they reminded him of the eyes of a bird.

He couldn't do this.

He wouldn't be the one pulling the lever that sent a man to his death. Not now. Not in front of Eleanor. He didn't want her to think of him as less than a man, even though all he really was now was the son of an executioner. Still, she didn't need to see this.

"Our Father, who art in Heaven…" Eleanor started praying out loud with the nuns, still staring at him with every word she spoke. Her rosary was gripped in one hand, and she wore a large crucifix on a chain around her neck. She wasn't dressed like a nun, but Connor couldn't be sure she hadn't joined the Order after all. He hoped for her sake that she hadn't. She deserved to be happy and to have a family with lots of children, like she'd always wanted. Like *they'd* always wanted.

"God's eyes, not the prayers again," grumbled Connor with clenched teeth.

The crowd became impatient. The nuns prayed even louder for the soul of the condemned man. Every time a group of nuns showed up at a hanging it made Connor feel twice as bad as he already did.

"Pull the damn lever!" shouted Lord Sampson from the crowd. He, of course, was the noble who had condemned this man to death. "Do it now, or I won't pay you, Wyland."

"Connor, do it," said his father, coughing even more. His face became pale. "Do it for me. I'm not feeling well and need to sit down."

Connor looked out at the crowd again, hearing the children crying, remembering the day he and his siblings cried and begged to have their father's life saved. All he wanted to do right now was to run over and cut the noose off the prisoner, and set him free.

But he couldn't.

To do that would mean he, as well as his father, would be killed in the man's place. His siblings at home would suffer because of it, if that were to happen. His first duty was to preserve his own family and to take care of their needs.

"Go," said his father, still coughing. He pushed Connor over to the lever. "It is your job."

His job.

His duty.

The words echoed in Connor's head feeling like the bony fingers of the devil probing and poking at his mind. He was sure he felt the fires of hell raging up within him. It was getting harder and harder to ignore the feeling of overwhelming doom.

This was Conner's awful, stinking, horrible life, and he hated it with every fiber of his being.

His eyes fixated on the lever. He supposed his father was right. He couldn't ignore this for much longer. Yes, he needed to learn to do what would be expected of him someday soon. There was no avoiding it anymore. Nervously reaching out, his hand wavered above the lever without touching it. Then he heard Eleanor cry out, and his gaze shot back to the crowd.

"You are doing the work of the devil and will burn in hell for taking the life of this woman's husband," shouted Eleanor. "How could you? Just look at her poor children. Do you want them to see this? Do you want this to be the last remembrance they have of their poor father?"

Connor swallowed deeply. Why did Eleanor's words have to feel like a knife to his gut? The more she spoke, the more the blade twisted inside him, deeper and deeper. He couldn't even look at the prisoner's wife or children now. It only reminded him too much of his own life, being a boy and about to see his own father killed. God's eyes, no one should have to go through this.

"Dammit, just do it!" growled his father in his ear. Then, before Connor knew what happened, his father's hand clamped over his, trapping it atop the lever of death. Connor's head snapped around, but too late. His father yanked Connor's hand and the lever was pulled. The floor under the prisoner's feet gave way, sending the condemned man to his death. When Connor's eyes shot back to the thief, he was gone. His feet were no longer on the platform, but now dancing on air.

Connor heard several women scream and then the shouts of the crowd as the dead man swung back and forth, his weight making the rope creak in the wind.

Part of the crowd cheered, happy to be rid of the thief. Then there were those who wailed and mourned for the man's life. The nuns prayed even louder. The dead man's widow dropped to her knees, clutching her children to her bosom as they all wailed and wept loudly.

Connor felt numb. As horrible as any execution was, he had taught himself over the past five years to dismiss his feelings when a man went to his death. Instead, he usually focused on anything else. Anything but his job. Over the years he was usually able to tamp down his emotions, or at least until the job was completed and the dead body had been hauled away and buried. Today, he was unable to do that. Not with Eleanor there glaring at him with those angry eyes, judging him, looking as if she wanted to kill him.

"How can you live with yourself after what you've just done?" snapped a nun from the foot of the gallows.

He didn't say a word.

"Dispose of the body," instructed his father. "I'm going to collect our pay from Sampson." His father left the platform.

Connor hunkered down and dug through his bag to find his sharp dagger that he used for cutting down the dead. His horse and cart were waiting near the gallows. So were the gravediggers who would assist him in burying the corpse. Connor had already paid Sampson's steward earlier, bribing him so Sampson wouldn't leave the dead man on view, but rather let him bury the man as soon as the hanging was over.

Connor couldn't bring himself to approach Sampson, since his hatred for the man was so strong. If he encountered him, there would be a risk of saying or doing something that might endanger his family. It bewildered him how his father could take money from the man, after it was he who ordered his father's death.

"You disgust me. You are heartless, despicable and... and... and you are an ogre." These words came from Eleanor this time. He looked up, his eyes meeting hers as she now stood with the nun at the foot of the platform. He never thought he'd hear the woman he was once supposed to marry saying these awful things to him. Especially since they had been so close during childhood. They were best friends. He and Eleanor had looked forward to their life as husband and wife. They'd even discussed the fact that they both wanted lots of children. It bothered him immensely that she seemed to hate him now, even if he deserved it. Still, it would do no good to show that her words cut him to the bone.

"I've been called worse," he answered softly, getting up and walking over to stare down at the deceased, swinging limply from the end of the rope through the hole in the platform. He could tell by the angle of the man's head that it was a clean break to his neck and that he'd died quickly. Connor nodded his approval and reached out and cut the man down. The prisoner's body fell with a thump to the ground beneath the gallows. Connor stuck his dagger through his belt, and made his way down the stairs, stopping only for a moment when he passed by Eleanor, looking back over his shoulder at her.

Was it wrong to want to gaze upon her beautiful face just once more? He couldn't stop thinking that this woman should be his wife right now and that he should be a respected knight, but he wasn't even close. Instead, he was feared and hated by all. People went out of their way to avoid him. He always heard gossip about him and his family as the crowds whispered behind his back.

His gaze traveled over to his past betrothed and once more he drank in her beauty. Eleanor's skin was smooth and pale—just like a noblewoman's was expected to be. She'd pulled her hood back up, but some loose tendrils of her vibrant red hair were still quite visible. It made her look like one of the mythical fae folk. Her rosewater scent drifted on the breeze, reminding him that she was no longer a girl like the last time he saw her. Now, she was a full-fledged woman. A woman who should be his... but wasn't.

"You'll regret this someday," the nun ground out, rushing away to comfort the widow. That left Connor standing alone with Eleanor. He couldn't even meet her gaze. He no longer had a right to look at her in this manner. Not when he was naught but a simple commoner—a bloody executioner, and she was a respected noblewoman.

He lowered his head and took a step away, but stopped suddenly when he felt her hand gently touch his arm.

"Connor, wait," came the sweet tone of her voice.

Flashes of memories filled his mind just from hearing her speak without the bitterness like before. It reminded him of many years ago, growing up with Eleanor at Saltwood Castle before she was sent to live at Marvane. They used to run through the hills during the summer, with him chasing her over the fields of green. He would tickle her until she begged for mercy. Then they would holds hands and stroll through fields of flowers as she sang and butterflies danced above their heads. Now, this seemed to him to be naught but a dream. Nothing but a different life, a different time when life was good and they were excited at what their future held. But it was only a dream, he reminded himself. One that he wanted to jump into and never return.

He turned slowly, his eyes fastening on Eleanor's slender fingers barely touching his forearm. Connor cursed inwardly, feeling a wave of excitement shoot up his spine from her mere gentle touch. He held his breath, his eyes roaming up her arm and to her face now. She was touching him. Actually touching him. What was she doing? He was an executioner, and no one ever touched him! It was thought to be a cursed thing to do, and was highly forbidden. As if she could read his thoughts, she gasped and slowly released her grasp, lowering her arm to her side.

"Your face," she whispered, having been there the day he received the mark of an executioner, but never having seen it until now. "I heard about it, but thought you'd be healed by now." Sadness filled her eyes and she turned and slowly looked away.

His hand shot up to cover his cheek where he'd been branded a hangman. He couldn't even bring himself to think of how ugly he looked to her right now. It made him want to hide his face from her. He didn't want her to see it. She most likely thought he was hideous now, when at one time she'd told him that he was very handsome.

"You shouldn't have touched me," he told her, barely able to speak. God's eyes, why had it felt so good to feel her hand on his arm? He had longed to be touched by Eleanor again, even if it was naught but in a friendly manner like in the past. It was all he could think about when he closed his eyes at night. And the fact that he'd never even gotten the chance to feel her lips pressed up against his made for many sleepless nights. Connor wanted nothing more than to pull her into his arms and kiss her right now, but sadly, that was never going to happen. "Now you're unclean and will probably be shunned for doing such a stupid thing," he told her. "Eleanor, what were you thinking?" His gaze dropped to the ground and shame washed over him.

"No one saw," came her sweet reply. "And touching you doesn't make me unclean or a bad person. You are a man, Connor. A man just like any other."

"Nay. I'm not just like any other man, Eleanor. How the hell can you even say that? You know what I am now," he said, looking out over the heads of the people who despised him, not able to face her anymore. "The burn on my face reminds anyone who might have forgotten."

"Connor, please. We don't have long. I had to see you. To talk to you. About what you're doing. It needs to stop."

This time, when he looked back at her face, those angry eyes he'd seen earlier were filled with tears. She seemed so sad that it about broke his heart.

"What is it you want me to do?" he asked, regretting being an executioner right now more than ever before. A stray strand of her hair blew across her face in the breeze, and he wanted more than anything to reach out and gently brush it back behind her ear.

But he wouldn't.

He couldn't touch her.

The fact that Eleanor had touched him willingly surprised him and somehow pleased him as well. Then again, it also made him angry, only reminding him of all that he'd lost. He hated and loved her action at the same time and confusion clouded his brain. Somehow, her touch seemed to awaken something within him that had died the day he'd had to walk out of his betrothed's life forever.

It wasn't just lust he felt for Eleanor right now, he realized. Nay, he had the whores on occasion to quench that urge. Instead, it was more. He'd felt the need to be touched again by someone who cared for him—or at least used to care. It hurt so much that it made him want to cry. Eleanor had been his best friend ever since they were children. He couldn't stop thinking about that lately. He also thought about his dear mother often —hugging him as a child and making him feel... loved. Yes, that was what was missing in his life right now, and something he'd most likely never have again in this lifetime.

"I want you to stop being a hangman," said Eleanor, making Connor shake his head and almost laugh aloud. If only it was that easy.

"You're a noblewoman, Eleanor," he reminded her. "You shouldn't be near me and certainly not be seen speaking with me. Go now, before you get in trouble."

"Connor, this isn't right. You shouldn't be putting people to death. You are a good and noble man. You have a kind heart and I know it. This isn't the life for you."

His head snapped up and he felt like shouting, but answered her with restraint. "Did you call me *noble*?" he repeated, blowing air from his mouth. "I might have been a noble at one time, but not anymore," he told her. "That was a different life then. But now, that life is over. I don't need you reminding me of something that has haunted me for the last five years."

"Walk away, please. Don't do this anymore. You are better than this." A tear dripped down her cheek, and once again he found himself wanting to touch her face, to brush the tear away the way he had done so long ago on that awful day.

"I can't, and you know it. Besides, why should you even care? You said I disgust you. I heard you call me heartless, despicable, and an ogre just moments ago." Once more, he looked away. It hurt too much to gaze upon her when he wanted her so badly. It especially hurt that he had let her down. That was the last thing he ever wanted to happen.

Eleanor sniffled and wiped away her tear with the back of her hand. Then she raised her chin and looked down her nose at him as she answered.

"Well, you are all those things, Connor. I'm sorry, but it's true! How could you pull the lever and send that poor woman's husband to his death?" Her arm shot out and she motioned toward the widow who was crying and still clutching her children.

"Me?" he asked in confusion. "Nay, Eleanor, I didn't pull the lever and kill that thief. My father did."

"I saw you do it, so stop lying! You will end up in hell for what you've done."

"I'm already in hell, sweetheart, so what does it even matter? I live in hell every day of my life. I'm sure you couldn't even begin to understand."

"Lady Eleanor, get away from that man!" shouted the abbess, rushing over and grabbing her arm, pulling her back. The nun looked cross. "Why are you even talking to the hangman? Get away from him, I say. No good can come of this." She made a big display of blessing herself over and over again.

"I needed to talk to him, Sister Sybil," said Eleanor. "This is the man I was once supposed to marry."

"May God have mercy on you, and forgive you for speaking with the man of death," gasped the nun, blessing herself yet again. "Let's go, Lady Eleanor. Your job is to comfort those in mourning, not to befriend the executioner who took the widow's husband from her."

"I-I need to go," Eleanor told Connor as the nun dragged her away from him. When she left, the wind blew her hood off her head again. The green ribbon tying back her hair came loose and fluttered to the ground at his feet. He reached down and picked it up, rubbing the smooth satin between his calloused fingers, wondering if her skin felt as soft. He found it hard to remember, and now would never know for sure.

"My lady. I think you dropped this," he called, holding the ribbon out to her like an offering of peace as it dangled between his fingers in the breeze, unfortunately not unlike the dead man who had been swinging from the rope just minutes ago.

"Keep it. She doesn't want it, now that you've touched it," said the nun, pulling Eleanor away.

Connor stood there holding on to Eleanor's hair ribbon, feeling like this was all he'd ever have of her. His heart was heavy, feeling like a weight in his chest. He watched Eleanor leave him, walking out of his life once again, the memory of that awful day playing through his mind once more. Then he looked down at the ribbon he now clutched in his hand, wanting to hold on to just this little memory of her, since it was all he'd ever have.

So close, and yet so far. He was being punished as God flaunted right in his face what Connor wanted most in life. Then it was whisked away from him, leaving him feeling even lonelier than before.

"Hangman, we're waiting for you," one of the gravediggers called out to him, leaning on his shovel.

Connor hated being called *hangman*. It sounded so dirty, so repulsive, and so unreal.

But that was what he was now, so what did he expect?

Shoving Eleanor's ribbon into his pouch, he turned his back to the crowd. He had a man to help bury. This job should be getting easier to accept by now, but today, it had only gotten so much worse.

CHAPTER 2

Connor closed up the back of his wagon as the gravediggers threw the last shovelfuls of dirt atop the thief that had been executed today. The man was buried in a prisoners' cemetery, far from the castle and on the outskirts of town. No one convicted of a crime and killed for it could be buried on holy ground.

He turned his head to see the church nearby. A graveyard next to it was enclosed by an iron fence. It was where his mother was buried. This made him wonder where he and his father would be buried once they died. He wasn't even sure a hangman was allowed to be buried amongst prisoners, and neither did he want to be.

"Connor, let's go," said his father, climbing aboard the wagon and taking the reins.

He spied Eleanor in the distance, leaving the gravesite with her arm around the grieving widow.

"Not yet," said Connor, brushing off his hands. "I want to stop and visit Mother's grave first."

"We're not allowed in the church graveyard and you know it." His father coughed a few more times.

"I'll be fast. No one will see me. Go on without me. I'll walk home."

"Walk?" asked his father. "That will take too long."

"I don't care. I need time alone to think."

"Don't be long. It's your turn to cook, and your brothers and sister will be hungry since they've been hunting all day."

"I'll be stopping by Francesca's grave on the way home, too," he said softly, feeling the void of his sister more and more every day. She'd died over the winter from the sweating sickness. His other siblings had been ill as well, but they'd recovered. Poor Francesca wasn't as lucky.

"The dead don't know if we come to visit or not," said his father. "Don't be wasting your time."

"When did you get so hard-hearted, to speak that way about your own wife and child?" snapped Connor, knowing his father hadn't been like this when Connor was little.

"I suppose, being around the dead so often, I've realized that once a person is gone, they're gone. There is no sense crying over it."

"At one time you never would have said such a thing," said Connor. "You killed because someone spoke badly of Mother once she passed away."

"That was a mistake and we both know it."

"Life is precious, but you don't seem to care anymore."

"I'm going home to lie down. Don't be long," said his father, slapping the reins against the horse and leaving. The creak of the cart wheels echoed in his ears. At one time they had used that wagon to bring the family on outings. His mother would pack up some food, and Connor and his siblings would hop in the back, happy to be spending time with their parents. They'd go to the lake and spread a blanket on the ground, and although nobles weren't supposed to see much sun, they'd lie down on the ground and look up at the clouds, never telling a soul what they did.

Aye, that wagon once represented love and happiness. Now, it was only used to haul the dead to their final resting place.

Connor turned and pulled his cloak closer around him, heading for the cemetery. He was so distraught today that he hoped talking to his deceased mother would help to ease his mind.

ELEANOR WAS ABOUT to get into the wagon with the nuns and start back to St. Anne's Abbey when she noticed Connor heading over to the cemetery. He was alone, and his father had already left. Her heart ached for him. She figured he was going to his mother's gravesite.

"Hurry up, Eleanor. We need to get back to the abbey," said her friend, Sister Barbara.

"Just give me a minute," she told them. "I need to make a quick visit to the cemetery first."

Eleanor hurried over to the cemetery, slipping inside the iron gate, looking for Connor. She was sure she saw him coming this way. Sure enough, she spotted him kneeling down at his mother's grave. She got closer and hid behind a gravestone, peeking out at him, hoping he didn't see her.

"Mother," she heard him say in a muffled voice. "This is for you. I know roses were always your favorite." He gently laid a single wild rose atop her grave. Still down on one knee, his head lowered, and Eleanor had to listen closely to hear what he had to say next. "Father is ill and it will not be long before he joins you. Then I will have to take his place as hangman."

The wind picked up, making it hard to hear. She had to step out a little, cocking her head and listening intently.

"I never wanted this. You know that," continued Connor.

When Eleanor moved, she stepped on a twig. It snapped, making a sound. Connor's head shot up and when it did, she didn't dare to move, let alone breathe. Then he continued without looking her way, but she swore he must have known she was watching when she heard his next words.

"I saw Eleanor today and she doesn't understand what I am going through. I hope she can forgive me and move on with her life. She doesn't realize that I have no choice in this matter."

Then, to her surprise, he turned his head and looked straight at her before she even had a chance to hide. His eyes held such sadness, mixed with a hint of danger, making her heart speed up. She wanted to say something to him, God knew she did. But she just couldn't bring herself to even speak a word, neither would she know what to say to help ease the man's pain.

Grasping her cloak around her, she turned and ran out of the cemetery without even looking back.

CONNOR STOOD at the gate to the cemetery, watching as Eleanor ran out and jumped into a wagon with the nuns. The horse started away as the sky became dark and the wind picked up even more. He had known she was there ever since she'd entered the cemetery. What was she doing? Why in heaven's name had she been watching him? Why couldn't she just leave him alone? His life was hard enough without her hanging around him. It only made him hate his new life even more.

He headed down the road for home just as it started to rain. He'd be soaked before long, but right now he didn't even care. Several wagons passed him on the road, and also a few men on horseback. None of them even offered him a ride, and neither did he bother to ask. Once they'd see his face, they would take off at full gallop atop their horses, leaving him in the dust, so he didn't even try.

It was a good hour's walk to his home from the castle. The sky opened up and a torrential downpour started. He stopped, removing his hood from his head and turning his face up to the sky with his eyes closed. Mayhap he'd be cleansed from the rains. Either that, or he'd catch pneumonia and die. Either way, he'd be free, he decided, so it didn't even matter. He walked in the rain all the way back, stopping in the woods near to his home where his sister Francesca was buried.

"Frannie," he said, pulling another wild rose from under his cloak, kneeling down at the pile of rocks that marked her grave. He placed the flower atop it, not even knowing what to say to his deceased sister. "I saw Mother," he whispered. "I know you are with her now. Father will be joining you soon. Or, mayhap not," he said, not sure he really believed in heaven and hell anymore. But if they really existed, his father's soul was sure to go in the opposite direction at death for the things he had done.

"Connor! Connor!" came the voice of a boy. When he looked up he saw his brother, Leoric of sixteen years, as well as his youngest brother, Alaric who was five. They made their way through the woods toward him. "Father said you'd be here. He wants you to come in out of the rain."

"Don't worry about me," he told his brothers, getting to his feet. "You two should stay dry. Alaric, where is your cape?"

"I left so fast that I forgot it," said the little boy.

"Here. Take mine," said Connor, removing his cloak and wrapping it around his little brother's shivering body.

"That cloak is too long. He'll trip," said Leoric.

"Not if I carry him. Alaric, get on my back. Hurry." Connor hunkered down and his youngest brother climbed on his back with the large cloak covering him as they all walked back to the cottage.

"What happened at the hanging today?" asked Leoric. "Father said something about you not wanting to do your job."

"Never mind," said Connor, not wanting to talk about the horrible day he had. Plus, he never discussed any of the executions with his siblings. There was no reason to do so. They didn't need the heavy burden he carried.

"Father said you didn't want to pull the lever. I would have pulled it," said Leoric. "Then the bloody thief would have gotten what he deserved." Leoric grabbed his throat and pretended to choke, hanging his head to the side. Alaric laughed at his brother.

"Stop it! Both of you," commanded Connor. "I don't ever want to hear you jest about someone's execution again."

"Well, if the man was guilty then he deserved to die," continued Leoric.

"Just like Father did?" asked Connor, shutting the boy up. "And believe me, if you were there, you wouldn't be so anxious to pull any lever."

Leoric scowled at Connor. "I want to go to the executions, but you never let me. I'm going to ask Father to take me next time instead of you, since you are too scared to do your job."

"Enough!" Connor spat. "Leoric, this kind of talk is unacceptable. Especially around Alaric."

"What difference does it make?" asked Leoric. "Once Father dies, you'll be the hangman. And when you die, I'll be the hangman. And if something happens to me too, then Alaric will have to do it someday. Unless one of us has a son first."

"Nothing is going to happen to me, so you two will never have to worry about being an executioner. Now stop all this talk immediately, because I don't want to hear it again. Did you make supper?"

"Ginevra made some soup, but it tastes like piss," said little Alaric from atop Connor's back.

"Soup?" asked Connor. "Nay, Father needs something more strengthening than that if he is going to heal his cough. And Ginevra is only eleven. Leoric, you should have helped her."

"Ginevra likes to cook, so I let her do it. We didn't have any fish or meat, only root vegetables," said Leoric as they approached the cottage.

"Didn't you hunt today?" asked Connor. Although hunting in the lord's forest was forbidden by commoners, the hangman was allowed to hunt once a month since he was banned from living in town. They had to collect all the meat they'd need for the month in one day and salt it and store it in the underground cellar out behind the house.

"I did, but I didn't catch anything. And now we're not allowed to hunt until next month," Leoric reminded him.

"Damn," said Connor, wishing he had been here to hunt since he would have been able to catch a deer or at least a few pheasants. He wondered if Lord Sampson's guards would really see him hunting if he decided to go out anyway in the dark. If nothing else, he could set a few snares and hopefully catch a hare or two by morning. Then again, if he was seen and imprisoned, what would happen to his siblings, and who would take care of his ailing father? Nay, he decided he couldn't risk it. Not right now. "I'll go to town in the morning and see if I can pick up an odd job or two to make some money to buy some meat at the butcher's."

"You know that no one in town will hire us," said Leoric.

"Well, I've got to try," said Connor. "I'm not just going to give up."

"I want to go to school to learn to read and write," said Alaric out of nowhere.

"Nay, Alaric," said Connor. "I told you, since we are the family of a hangman, none of us are allowed in school. I or Leoric will teach you instead."

"Father said you saw Eleanor," said Leoric, changing the conversation once again. "I remember her. She was nice. And pretty."

"Who is Eleanor?" asked Alaric, as they approached the house. Connor put his youngest brother down.

"She's Connor's betrothed," Leoric told him. "That means they are getting married."

"Nay," said Connor. "She used to be my betrothed, but not anymore. We will never get married now." He opened the door and they entered the cottage to find their father bent over the table wrapped in a blanket. Little Ginevra was holding a spoon with soup on it up to his mouth.

"Connor!" Ginevra put the spoon back in the bowl and ran over to hug him. "I'm glad you're home."

"Don't hug me, Sister. I am too wet from the rain," Connor told her, removing the wet cloak from around Alaric.

"I'm hungry," complained Alaric, climbing atop a stool, reaching for the pot in the center of the table.

"You already had soup," Ginevra scolded him. "We need to save some for Connor and Father."

"I'm not hungry. Alaric can have mine," said Connor, feeling his stomach growling.

"Alaric, I thought you said my soup tasted like piss." Ginevra crossed her arms over her chest and glared at her younger brother.

"It does. But I don't care. I'm hungry," said Alaric, always having an appetite. Connor was sure the little boy was going to grow taller than him someday.

"I'll go hunt," offered Connor, but his father stopped him.

"Nay, Connor. We can't risk you being caught by one of Sampson's guards.

"Then I'll go to town and find something for us to eat there."

"The money is all gone," said Leoric.

"Nay, it can't be. We were paid for a hanging today," said Connor, looking over at his father.

His father lowered his face to the table, not looking at Connor. "Use the coin the thief paid us at the hanging, Son."

"I-I can't," said Connor, running a hand through his long, wet hair and looking the other way.

"Why the hell not?" growled Wensel, his body shivering under the blanket. He pulled out a wineskin that Connor knew contained whisky and took a long swig.

"I gave the coin back to the thief's widow," explained Connor, knowing his father wasn't going to like hearing this.

"Why the hell would you do such a daft thing?" yelled Wensel, the uproar sending him into a coughing fit.

"The poor woman had two children to raise," said Connor softly.

"And I've got five," snapped Wensel, taking another swig of whisky. "So what's the difference?"

"Four children, Father," Ginevra corrected him. "Remember, there are only four of now, since Francesca died."

"We needed that money," said Wensel, shaking his head. "If you could stop spending our coins on whores, mayhap we wouldn't be going hungry."

"You did?" asked Leoric, his eyes growing wide, suddenly interested in this bit of information.

"I didn't use the coins on whores," said Connor, throwing his brother a dirty look. "I've been giving the money back to the deceased ones' families, as well as paying off the lord or steward of the castle not to put the corpses on display."

"Damn you, Connor, no wonder we are so broke," spat his father, coughing some more, taking another swig of whisky.

"If you would stop spending our coin on whisky for yourself and start taking care of your family for once, mayhap we wouldn't be in this predicament," snapped Connor.

His father's dark eyes bore into him, and held a dangerous look that Connor had never really seen before.

"Why do you think I drink so much whisky?" he asked, answering his own question before Connor could respond. "Do you think I am so heartless and emotionless that a hanging or decapitating a man doesn't even bother me? Well, do you?" he shouted. His eyes held fire. The room suddenly became quiet. No one spoke or even moved.

"None of this had to be," Connor finally told him. "If only you had made your own decision instead of making me do it that day." His father knew damned well Connor meant the day he made the decision to save his father's life. He knew, but he would never admit he'd made a mistake. Not really.

"That's enough!" His father stood up so fast that he spilled the soup, sending what little food they had flowing across the table. "I'm going to bed. I need my rest and do not want to be disturbed. Do you all understand me?" Once again, he lifted the wineskin, drinking down his coveted whisky.

"Yes, Father," said Alaric, followed by nods from Ginevra and Leoric. Then he dug into his pouch and threw a shilling on the table with a loud clank. The coin spun around faster and faster, finally falling and becoming still. "Find something for them to eat, Connor," he commanded, turning and heading toward the bedroom.

The cottage was small, but did have two rooms besides the main eating area. Connor's family had built it themselves. Their father occupied one of the bedrooms, while Ginevra and Alaric used the other. Leoric and Connor slept on pallets in the main room of the house.

Once the door slammed shut, Connor found his siblings all staring at him, waiting for him to say something.

"Ginevra, clean up the spilled soup," said Connor, scooping the coin off the table. "The rest of you, eat as much as you want, because I won't be having any." He picked up his wet cloak and put it around his shoulders.

"Where are you going?" asked Leoric. "Father said not to hunt."

"I'm not," answered Connor. "I'll be taking the horse, and will return sometime tomorrow." He headed for the door.

"You're taking the horse?" asked Leoric, shaking his head. "Nay. What if Father has another hanging and needs the wagon?"

"There are no hangings scheduled for tomorrow. Besides, we are always given at least two days' notice, so don't worry. I'll be back by then, and I'll bring food." He looked at the single shilling in his hand, knowing this wasn't enough to buy much, and certainly not enough to feed an entire family for even one day. They were paid five shillings for a hanging. The lords demanded two shillings from Connor not to display the bodies but to let him bury them instead. Plus, Connor usually gave any money from the convicted back to the family. That left three shillings, but his father had probably spent half of that before they even left the castle, buying whisky for himself from one of the guards. And if he gambled any of it away, that left even less for the family.

"I want biscuits," said Alaric, running his finger through the spilled soup on the table and licking his finger afterwards.

"I want sweetmeats," said Ginevra.

"Sweetmeats?" asked Leoric. "We haven't had that since we left the castle." His tongue shot out and he licked his lips, looking like he was salivating just thinking of the candied fruit.

"Well, I like them," Ginevra continued.

"I'm sorry, but there won't be any sweetmeats," said Connor, putting the shilling in his pouch. Since sweetmeats weren't something that pitiful poor commoners like themselves would ever have the pleasure of eating again, he didn't even want to get his sister's hopes up.

"Then I want seedcake like Francesca used to make," said his sister. "I miss Francesca. And I miss Mother too." She lowered her head, using a rag to slowly clean up the spilled soup.

"We all do," said Connor. "However, wishing for them won't bring them back. We need to move ahead, not get stuck in the past."

"Then bring me whisky," said Leoric. "I tried some of Father's once when he wasn't here, and I liked it."

"Stay away from the whisky," Connor warned him.

"I only had a little. Father never even knew," said his brother.

"One sip is how it all starts. I don't want you ending up like our father. Now, lock the door behind me and don't any of you go outside until morning," Connor instructed.

"What about Father?" asked his sister.

"What about him?" Connor looked back over his shoulder.

"What if he should die before you return?"

"I don't want Father to die," wailed Alaric.

"Don't worry, he'll be fine." Connor ruffled the little boy's hair.

Sadly, part of him wished his father would die. Connor couldn't stand seeing the man he once admired—the noble, respected knight—turn into nothing but a mean drunk and murderer, hated and feared by all. Then again, another part of him truly feared the man's death. Because once that happened, Connor's life of hell would only get worse, having to take over as the hangman.

CHAPTER 3

The rain let up, and Eleanor found herself still feeling shaken as well as anxious later that day. It wasn't only from having attended the hanging, but also because of seeing Connor once again. She walked through the courtyard of St. Anne's Abbey holding the hands of Margaret and Lena, two of the orphan girls who were two and four years of age. Seven-year-old Bertram and five-year-old Hamlin followed right behind her.

Eleanor had dedicated her time helping out at the abbey. While she didn't feel the need to take her vows and become a nun, she also hadn't been able to bring herself to get married if the man wasn't Connor. After her betrothal to Connor had been broken five years ago, she felt so disheartened that she told her parents she needed to be of service at the abbey instead of being betrothed to another man. Thankfully, her mother, who used to be a pirate, was able to convince her father to give her the time she needed to be healed from this traumatic event.

"I'm scared," said little Hamlin from behind. "I don't want to leave here, Lady Eleanor."

"Well, I do," said Bertram, who was much too old to even be there anymore.

Eleanor's job was to tend to the orphans, and to help find them good homes amongst the commoners, where they could live and help work the land or the business, if the families were merchants. Unfortunately, she had become so attached to the children that she hadn't really been looking hard for families for them lately. However, in the past few days, she came across a farmer and his wife who had recently lost their sons to sickness. They were ready to take in not just one, but both of the boys.

Eleanor stopped and turned around to face the boys.

"Edna and Albert Woods are wonderful people and very kind," she told the boys. "They recently lost two sons to sickness and need your help plowing and planting the fields."

"I can do the work of a man," bragged Bertram, even though they all knew it was a lie.

"Mayhap someday that will be true," she told the boy. "But for now, it'll take both of you to make a difference in their farming."

"I'll miss you." Hamlin barreled into her, almost knocking her down, throwing his arms around her. She released the hands of the girls and hunkered down to hug the little boy.

"You know that I will visit often. And if you are unhappy for any reason at all, you can tell me. I'll be checking up on how you're doing at least once a week."

"Are we leaving too?" asked Margaret, reaching out and taking Lena's hand. They were all like siblings, even though as far as Eleanor knew, none of them were really related. The boys had been orphaned three years ago when a sickness spread through the village killing their families. Both of the girls had been babies dropped off at the door of the abbey, most likely by parents who could no longer care for them. Usually, the families kept the boys to help with the work, but the girls were not valued as much.

"Nay, Margaret. You and Lena will stay here for now. But someday, you will have families to live with as well."

"Mother," said little Lena, looking up with big blue eyes, breaking free of Margaret and clinging to Eleanor. The girls had never known another mother, and considered Eleanor the one to fill that position. She actually enjoyed it and felt as if they were her children. It broke her heart every time one of the orphans was placed with a family and left the abbey. Still, she knew it was what was best for them.

"Lady Eleanor, Mr. and Mrs. Woods are here for the boys," said Sister Barbara, who often helped Eleanor care for the orphans. She had also become a good friend of Eleanor's over the years.

"It's time," said Eleanor, kissing Hamlin on the head and standing up. "Sister Barbara, will you watch over the girls? I will take the boys to meet their new parents."

"Of course," said the nun, taking the hands of both the girls.

"Come along, Bertram," said Eleanor, holding Hamlin's hand so the boy wouldn't be scared and run. "I want both of you to be respectful of Mr. and Mrs. Woods. Do you understand? Treat them no different than you would me."

"I wonder if I'll have my own room," said Bertram. "Or if Mrs. Woods will bake pies and cakes. I like pies and cakes."

"So do I," said Hamlin, his interest suddenly piqued. "But I'm scared."

"There is no need to be frightened," Eleanor assured them. "Bertram will be with you, and you two will be brothers now."

"What about Margaret and Lena?" asked Hamlin. "They are our sisters."

"I will be sure to bring them by for visits."

"Ah, there you are," said the abbess, standing at the side of a wagon with Mr. and Mrs. Woods. "Come along, boys. Get in the wagon. There is work to be done back at their farm."

The Woods were serfs who were bound to Lord Sampson, farming his land. They had to pay him taxes as well. However, they did have a plot of land that was their own. They were the poorest of peasants, and worked hard to make a living. Eleanor's heart went out to peasants. She always tried to help them as best she could. Albert had been skeptical about taking both the boys, but Eleanor talked him into it, since his wife wanted them both badly. Eleanor also felt it would be an easier transition for Hamlin if he would stay with Bertram, since he was the more sensitive of the two. She also promised to help the family out financially as much as she could, whenever it was possible.

"Hello there," said Edna Woods, a round, plump lady with a big smile on her face. "Which one of you is Bertram and which is Hamlin?" she asked.

"I'm Bertram," the older boy said, standing up straighter, acting very proud. "I'm seven but Hamlin is only five."

"My dear, these boys are so small and very young," Albert told his wife softly. "This might be more of a burden than a help to us right now."

"Oh, nay, I assure you, these boys will be more than helpful," Eleanor told the couple. "As a matter of fact, they've already been quite the help in the orchards here at the abbey, picking fruit."

"That's fine, but we don't have orchards," grumbled Albert. "We farm the lord's land. Our boys helped me plow and plant the wheat. These two are too young to do that."

"Albert, please," said Edna, looking like she was about to cry.

"I'm really strong," said Bertram, stepping up to them. "I'm also almost eight. Did Lady Eleanor tell you that? I can be a lot of help. I know everything about planting and harvesting crops."

"Do you, now?" said Albert, not seeming at all convinced.

"Bertram knows how to read," said Eleanor. "And I've been teaching him to write as well."

"Really?" Albert's head popped up. Peasants didn't have either of these skills.

"Did you hear that, dear?" whispered Edna. "We can't read or write, so he might be a good asset to us after all. Especially at harvest time when we sell some of our own crops."

"Well, I guess it'll be all right. But I don't see why we need both of them. That is just another mouth to feed."

"Mr. Woods," said the abbess. "It seems Lady Eleanor has made a bad decision. I suggest you only take the older boy."

"Nay! I didn't make a mistake," said Eleanor, knowing how badly Edna wanted both boys. She had spoken to Eleanor for hours about it. She lost two sons, and the only thing that was going to help her get through this was if she had two boys to fill the void. Plus, Eleanor wanted the boys to stay together.

"Please, Albert," whispered Edna, wringing her hands. "I know our sons are gone now and can never be replaced, but this will hopefully help me to be able to stop my grieving."

"She's right," said Eleanor. "And Bertram and Hamlin are already like brothers, so it would be sad to split them up."

"I agree," said Edna, her eyes roaming over to little Hamlin. "Are you hungry, Hamlin?" she asked.

"We like pies. And cakes," said Hamlin. "Do you know how to make them?"

"Why, yes, I do," said the woman. "However, we farm vegetables and don't have a lot of fruit for pastries."

"I'll be sure to send plenty of apples and pears from the orchards here at the abbey," promised Eleanor, getting a scowl from the abbess, but she didn't care. Her father had enough money that Eleanor would pay for the fruit herself if needed.

"What do you say about all this?" the abbess asked Albert.

"Well, I guess it would be nice to have two boys back in the house again. However, I want to make it clear that they will never take the place of our sons, Alfred and Simon."

"Of course not, Mr. Woods," said Eleanor. "And neither does anyone expect that. But in time, I am sure you will all feel like a family again."

"Get in the wagon, boys," said Albert, with a nod of his head.

"Can I ride up front and hold the reins?" Bertram was climbing up on the bench seat of the wagon before Albert could even answer.

"Mayhap he will be more help than I thought," said Albert with a shrug, hurrying over to the wagon.

"Hamlin, come with me," said Edna, holding out her hand to the little boy. Hamlin was reluctant, still clinging to Eleanor.

"It's all right. Go with her," said Eleanor, bending over and giving the boy a kiss on the cheek.

"Do I have to ride in the back all by myself?" asked Hamlin, looking frightened. Just then, a dog stuck his head up over the side of the wagon. "Is that a dog?"

"Why, yes, that is Roger, our dog. Would you like to pet him?" asked Edna.

"Would I!" Hamlin took off at a run for the wagon with Edna right behind him.

"Lady Eleanor," said the abbess.

"Yes?" asked Eleanor.

"I have had several complaints lately from the townspeople about that boy Finnian, whom you placed with the butcher a few years ago."

"Finnian? What about him?"

"It seems he is causing a lot of trouble. There are reports that he has been stealing from some of the townsfolk."

"Oh, no. That is not good. I will ride out to town immediately and talk to Finnian and also his family, and see why this is happening. I'll take the horse and wagon, and drop off some apples for Mrs. Woods to make pies since I'll be going right past their cottage on the way."

"They are just leaving," said the abbess, watching them go. "You can have them take the apples with them now."

"Nay, I think I'd like to stop by just to make sure Hamlin is getting settled and isn't frightened."

"Lady Eleanor, you are too attached to these orphans," scolded the abbess. "It's not right."

"They all feel as if they are my own children," said Eleanor.

"But they're not. They are just orphans of commoners," the strict nun reminded her. "You are a noble, and need to find a nobleman to marry and have a family of your own."

"I mean no disrespect, Sister Sybil, but it is really none of your business what I do," said Eleanor, hating how the nun seemed to judge her.

"You need to stop waiting around for that executioner, because it looks bad for you and your family."

"I never said I was," she protested.

"Hrmph," spat the nun, sticking her hands under her mantle and turning away. "Be sure to take one of the monks with you to town. You cannot go unescorted."

"I'll be back before dark," she told the abbess, letting out a deep sigh.

"What was that all about?" asked Sister Barbara, hurrying

over, holding the hands of the girls. Both Lena and Margaret waved to the boys as the Woods' wagon pulled away. Little Hamlin was in the back with his arm around the dog, smiling from ear to ear.

"I am going to town for a while, Sister Barbara. I'll be taking the horse and wagon."

"And one or two of the monks as well, for protection?" asked the nun, already knowing that Eleanor had no intention of doing such a thing. St. Anne's Abbey was headed by the abbess, but they had a chapter house with monks and laymen who helped out with the heavy work and in the orchards and fields.

"Keep the abbess busy while I am gone," said Eleanor, never answering so she wouldn't have to lie, and not wanting to put Sister Barbara in an uncomfortable position. Eleanor didn't feel that she would be in danger traveling alone, since she wouldn't be going that far. She also wasn't going to the rough parts of town. The butcher was at the edge of town, so she'd pay her visit and then head back before the sun went down.

It wasn't long before Eleanor directed the horse away from the abbey, being sure the abbess didn't see her leave unescorted. In the back of the wagon she had three bushels of apples. She figured she'd leave two with Edna and give the last one to the butcher, hopefully convincing him not to send Finnian back to the abbey. Finnian was nearly thirteen now, and had been more trouble than all the other orphans put together. She had known the boy had a habit of stealing, but never told Tom the butcher, or his wife Alice, because if she had, she was afraid no one would ever take the boy. He had been ten when she finally found a family for him, and she had hoped his stealing was only done for attention and that it would end when he had parents to give him what he needed.

Well, it looked like she was wrong, and she wasn't sure what to do.

She was nearing the village when the wheel of the wagon got caught in a rut in the road. The rain had made the road rougher than usual, but she hadn't realized it until now.

"Oh, no!" she said, climbing down from the wagon. Sure enough, the wheel was stuck in a deep rut and she wasn't sure how to get it out. Reaching over the side of the wagon, she grabbed an apple and gave it to the horse, petting the animal behind the ears. "You stay put while I try to figure out what to do." She immediately regretted not bringing along a monk or two with her.

Holding up her gown, she tried to avoid the muddy puddles, making her way to the back of the wagon.

"Mayhap I can give it a push," she said, putting her hands on the back of the wagon. When she did, her foot sank down into the muddy rut, ruining her shoes and the bottom of her gown. "Nay," she moaned, letting out a deep sigh. Her hand went to the gold cross hanging from a chain around her neck and she silently prayed to God for help.

"Can I help you, my lady?" came a deep voice from behind her. She jumped in surprise, turning so fast that she lost her balance when her shoe stuck fast in the mud.

"Oh!" she cried, falling. But before she could hit the ground, two strong arms of a man caught her, picking her up and carrying her to the side of the road.

She panicked.

"Put me down! Release me at once," she shouted to the hooded man, thoughts swarming in her head that this might be a ruffian wanting to have his way with her. She reached for her dagger at her side, and raised it up quickly, causing the man to jerk back his head so he wouldn't be cut. When he did, his hood fell, revealing his face.

"Be careful with that blade, Eleanor. You're going to hurt someone."

She froze, her eyes opening wide to see the scarred face of Connor.

"C-Connor?" she said, feeling her heart about beating out of her chest. She wasn't sure if it was fear from possibly being raped, or excitement at discovering she was in Connor's strong arms.

He instantly put her on her feet.

"I saw you were having trouble and only wanted to help." He held up his hands and backed away. "I am sorry that I touched you."

"Nay, don't be," she said, tears filling her eyes as she shook her head. "Thank you for your help." She looked down to see her muddy gown. "I think I lost my shoe in the rut."

"I'll retrieve it for you, my lady." He was back in a second with her muddy shoe. Down on his knees, he reached out for her foot, then suddenly stopped and looked up at her. "If I may?" His dark eyes stared up at her as he waited for her permission.

Eleanor studied his face this close up, drinking in his handsome looks. His long brown hair was wet, probably from the rain. It hung down to his shoulders. Strong cheekbones and the slight hook of his nose led to a short beard and mustache. She found herself wondering if he was trying to hide the burn mark on his cheek that had scarred him and pointed out the fact that he was an executioner.

With one shaky hand, she reached out, not able to stop herself from gently running her fingers along his cheek, tracing the mark that branded him as a man to be feared and avoided at all costs. The jagged line was raised and held a silvery tint. It felt leathery and not at all as soft as the rest of his cheek. She saw his eyes close when she touched him. He seemed to hold his breath and pressed his lips together hard. She swore she felt his body trembling.

"I'm so sorry, Connor," she whispered, and when she did, his eyes popped back open.

"Your foot, my lady," he said, quickly lowering his face to the ground.

She gave him her foot and he put the muddy shoe onto it. It didn't feel good but it also didn't matter. Her discomfort, she was sure, was nothing compared to what this poor man had been through.

Before she could say more, he jumped up and trudged through the mud, putting his hands on the back of the wagon. "I'm sure I can free this but I'll need you to walk the horse forward while I push."

"Oh, of course." She hurried to the front of the wagon.

"Take the reins from inside the wagon so you won't have to walk in the mud anymore."

She did as he instructed. With Connor pushing, the wheel was easily freed from the mud.

"It worked! Thank you," she said, looking over her shoulder at him.

"You shouldn't be out without an escort," he told her, sounding as if he were truly concerned. "These roads aren't safe. What were you thinking?"

"I travel by myself all the time," she told him, as he walked up to the side of the cart. "I just wasn't expecting to get stuck in the mud, that's all. I suppose it was a bad decision to come alone after all."

"Where are you going?" he asked, curiously.

"I'm stopping by a peasants' home to drop off apples from the abbey's orchard. I've just placed two of the orphans there as their new home," she told him. "Then I'm going to town to check on another orphan who seems to be causing trouble."

"Nay." He looked down the road and shook his head. "You can't go to town by yourself. You'll need to find an escort."

"Well, I don't have an escort, and I am not about to go back to the abbey to find a monk. I'll waste too much time. It will be dark before I finish."

"Then I'll escort you myself," he told her.

"You?" Her heart jumped into her throat.

"Don't worry, no one will know I'm with you." He pulled his hood up to cover his head. "I'll walk behind the wagon, and be here if you should encounter any trouble."

"Nay. I won't hear of it," she told him adamantly.

"I understand," he said, lowering his face and shaking his head. "Then I suppose I'll be on my way. I'm sorry to have disturbed you." He started down the road.

"Nay, Connor, wait," she called out, directing the horse and catching up with him. "I meant, I won't have you following behind me like a dog. I want you to escort me, but I want you to ride inside the wagon. Not walk behind me. I want you to ride up on the bench seat with me."

He stopped and looked up in surprise. She stopped the horse as well.

"I-I can't do that and you know it."

"No one needs to know it is you. They'll just think you are my escort."

"You realize that if anyone realizes who I am, you'll be shunned and chastised. I can't risk that happening. You don't deserve it."

"And you don't deserve the treatment you get, either. I won't let you walk to wherever it is you are going. Now get in. I won't hear another word about it."

"Nay, Eleanor. Don't ask me to—"

"Do it!" she commanded, seeming to surprise him so much that he didn't object again.

"All right," he said, climbing up to the bench seat and sitting next to her. "But when you approach your peasants' cottage or town, I will get out and stay in the shadows until you are finished with your visits."

"So be it," she said, traveling down the road again. They rode for a while without talking, and finally she broke the awkward silence between them. "Where are you headed on foot?"

"I am going to town to try to find some food for my family."

"Your family? Are you... married?"

"Nay," he said looking at her from the corners of his eyes. "No one would marry a hangman. I speak of my siblings and father only."

"Oh." More silence. "Aren't you going to ask if I'm married?"

"You're not," he said, sounding so sure of himself.

"What makes you think that?"

He chuckled. "Two reasons. First of all, no nobleman worth his salt would let a beautiful wife like you travel unescorted." He looked over at her, and she felt as if her tongue were too big for her mouth. She couldn't even respond to that. He'd called her *beautiful*. The last time she heard that from any male was when she was twelve and betrothed to Connor. He'd told her that once or twice when they were children, but it never meant anything up until that point. Now, since they were both adults, it meant even more.

"What is the second reason?" she asked, wanting to know how he knew about her when she knew basically nothing about him anymore.

"I saw you with nuns and you wear an ornate golden cross on a chain around your neck. That brings me to believe you either are training to be a nun, or spend a lot of time at the abbey."

69

"What makes you think I'm not already a nun?"

"Dressed like that? You are wearing the gown of a noble, not a habit. Nay, I don't think so, sweetheart."

Why in heaven's name did his simple endearment of calling her *sweetheart* make her feel so warm?

"You're right. I'm not married." Eleanor felt like a fool for asking him that last question. For some reason, just being around him made it hard for her to think or speak properly.

"Why not?" he asked her.

"Why not what?" she replied.

"Why didn't you ever get married? You are a beautiful, smart woman who seems to care for others. Your family has money, your father is Lord Warden of the Cinque Ports, and you are of childbearing age."

"I'm only nineteen, Connor."

"Most girls have several children by now."

"True. But I am not most girls."

"Nay, I guess not."

When she looked back at him, his intense eyes were drinking her in and it felt a little dangerous. Then again, she was sitting all alone next to a man whose occupation was to kill people, so why should she feel any differently?

"If you must know, I decided to dedicate myself to helping orphaned children find homes. Families to live with. I've been living at the abbey for a while now."

"You sound as if you're hiding from something. Are you?"

"I'm not hiding," she said softly, feeling very sad.

"Bid the devil, Eleanor, you're not waiting for me, are you? Please tell me that is not so."

"What?" she asked in surprise. How did he know this? Then again, Connor always seemed to know what she was thinking long before she ever told him. When they were just children, he could tell when she was keeping something from him. He even guessed the answer the time when she had borrowed his favorite eating knife without asking, trying to stab and catch a fish in the lake. She lost it in the water, and they never found it.

Eleanor smiled inwardly, realizing that some things never changed. "Nay, of course not. I wasn't waiting for you," she told him, trying to sound believable. "I just didn't want to get married, that's all." She squeezed her eyes closed for a moment, trying to ignore the fact she'd just lied to the only man she'd ever loved. He had to know she wanted marriage and many children more than anything, since they'd talked about it often when they were betrothed.

"Good," he answered, thankfully not calling her on her lie. "Because, we both know that we can never be together. Not anymore, since my father took the position of hangman to save his life."

"Yes," she said, barely able to breathe now. All she'd been able to think about every day for the past five years is getting Connor back. But he was right. It was never going to happen.

"Don't waste your life, Eleanor. Marry a nobleman right away and make something of yourself. You have so much to offer."

"I feel that I *am* making something of myself," she retorted. "I have helped dozens of orphaned children who had no one, and now they have loving families, thanks to me. As a matter of fact, here is my first stop. If you'll excuse me, I need to take some apples to the peasants who just took in two of my orphan boys today."

"Your boys," he repeated softly, telling her that he knew her secret. She thought of these children as her own, since she hadn't bore any from her own womb.

Eleanor stopped the wagon and hopped off. By the time

71

she got to the back of it, Connor was already there, pulling out a bushel of apples with his two strong arms.

"Are all three bushels going to the peasants?" he asked.

"Nay," she answered, about to say *two of them*, but she changed her mind at the last minute. "Just one. And I can carry it, but thank you." She held out her arms and waited.

"Nay. I'll carry it. I'll leave my hood up and they won't know who I am," he told her. "Unless you'd rather I hide if you're afraid they might find out."

"Nay, I'm not afraid. Thank you for carrying the bushel for me."

CONNOR FOLLOWED ELEANOR, carrying the basket of apples to the cottage, where two young boys were playing with a dog outside. A plump woman was sprinkling feed for a dozen chickens and looked up as they approached.

"Lady Eleanor, we just left you at the abbey," said the woman with a smile. "I didn't expect to see you again so soon."

"Lady Eleanor," shouted the younger boy, running over to her for a hug. The little white dog barked and followed, with the older boy right behind.

"Hamlin, I know how much you were hoping for an apple pie, so I brought a bushel of apples so your new mother can bake one. Edna, I hope these will do."

"Oh, apples, how wonderful!" said the woman. "Thank you. You can put them down over there." Her gaze traveled over to Connor as he walked away, and she leaned in and spoke softly to Eleanor, but Connor could still hear her. "Who is this man helping you? He doesn't look like a monk." Connor glanced back over his shoulder, seeing the woman craning her neck, trying to peek at Connor's face under his hood.

He started to regret his decision to carry the apples when

the peasant woman started asking questions that he didn't want answered.

"He's my escort," was all Eleanor said, and it seemed to satisfy the woman, for now, anyway.

"Just leave the bushel there by the front door and I'll have Albert carry them inside," Edna called out to him.

"I'm strong. I can carry them." The older boy ran over and grabbed the bushel, and at the same time looked up at Connor's face. From his short height, he could see him. The boy's eyes opened wide and he balked.

"It's all right," Connor told him in a soft voice. "I am here to protect Lady Eleanor."

"But you're a—"

"Shhhh," said Connor, his eyes flashing over to the others who were talking and not paying attention to him, thank goodness. "Take the apples for your new mother."

"Yes, sir," said the boy, as if he were afraid to say no.

"What's your name?" asked Connor.

"I'm Bertram."

"Thank you, Bertram. I can see why Lady Eleanor is so fond of you."

"I'll take that," said a man, emerging from the house and walking toward them.

"Don't say anything. Please," whispered Connor.

The little boy nodded in agreement, taking the bushel of apples from Connor, and turning to give them to Albert. Connor turned and hurried back to the wagon.

"I have to leave now, but I'll be back soon to visit," he heard Eleanor tell the others. "Goodbye."

"Thank you again," shouted Edna, waving her arm in the air. The boys started playing with the dog once again.

Connor was already in the wagon with the reins in his hand by the time Eleanor got there.

"My, you're in a hurry," she said, settling herself on the seat next to him. "Are you going to drive?"

"Yes," he said, slapping the reins against the horse. The horse took off down the road.

"Where are the rest of the apples going?" he asked her.

"I need to stop at the butcher's next."

"Oh," he said, not sounding happy about it. "I think when we get to town, I'll walk and meet up with you when you're finished."

"I thought you said you were coming to town to get food for your family. Were you planning on stopping at the butcher's at all?" she asked so innocently that it almost made him laugh.

"Nay, Eleanor. One shilling isn't going to buy enough meat for anyone."

"Oh, I'm sorry."

"Don't be. I'm a commoner now. Commoners don't usually eat a lot of meat."

"So, your family never has meat?" she asked.

Conner's stomach growled just thinking of the stuffed swan or thick slices of venison in gravy that he used to eat often at the castle. They were his favorite.

"The only meat we have is what we are allowed to hunt in Lord Sampson's forests. But that is only once a month and I missed it since I had to attend the hanging. Now, I have to wait a whole month before I can hunt again."

"Really? That is too long."

"It's the rules."

"Well, what were you planning on buying in town with just a shilling?"

"I don't know. I was hoping to stop by the baker's shop and see if he's got any old bread."

"Conner, this isn't right. You have noble blood and should

74

be eating like those who sit above the salt, not below it," she told him.

"Nay, you're wrong," he said, stopping the horse at the edge of town. "I'm not a noble. Not anymore." He handed her the reins and jumped off the wagon.

"Come with me."

"I can't. It's too risky. Someone in town might recognize me." He looked up and eyed the sun getting low in the sky. Dark clouds were blowing in. "Make your visit a fast one and meet me back here quickly. It's going to storm again soon. I want to make sure you're back safely at the abbey before that happens."

"But Connor—"

"Just do it," he said, walking away, trying not to be seen with her.

Since it was getting late in the day, by the time Connor got to the baker's shop, it was already closed. He turned and headed toward the seedier part of town, knowing it was his only hope of getting any kind of food for his family yet today. He was just about up to the tavern when a boy shot out of a dark passageway, crashing into him.

"Oomph," said Connor, as the air was knocked from his lungs.

"Sorry," said the boy, glancing up for just a second. When he saw the burn mark on Connor's face, he gasped.

"It's all right. No harm done," said Connor, flashing the boy a smile and holding up his palms. The boy took off like a bat out of hell. Connor continued walking to the tavern, stopping outside when he saw Lilith, one of the regular whores he'd paid for on occasion when he had an itch to scratch.

"Executioner," she said, without even having to see his face.

"Don't call me that, Lilith. You know I hate it."

"Are you here to see me?" she asked with a smile, walking over to him and running her hand down his chest.

"Nay, I'm not," he told her. "I'm here to get food for my family only."

"Mayhap you'll have an extra hay'penny for me?" she tried once again, offering her services.

"Nay, Lilith, not tonight." His hand went down to his pouch. "I only have enough—oh hell, where is my pouch?" He grabbed at the strings that had held it to his belt, seeing that they'd been cut.

"Looks like you were robbed," said the girl, staring at his waist. "Excuse me, I think I see a customer who can actually pay." She turned to go.

"Lilith, wait. Is there any way you can get me some food for my family?"

"What do I look like, hangman? I'm a whore, not a damned nun. I don't do charity for anyone, not even you."

"Damn it," he spat, running a hand through his hair. "The boy," he said aloud, knowing now that the boy from the passageway had robbed him and he'd never even known it. He looked up and down the street, trying to find the thief but didn't see him anywhere. "God's eyes, can this day get any worse?" he grumbled through gritted teeth, heading back to the spot where he was to meet Eleanor—the woman he would always love but would never have.

CHAPTER 4

"Thank you for the apples," said Tom, the butcher, unloading them from the back of Eleanor's wagon. "I see you have one more bushel. Do you have another stop to make yet?"

"Yes. Yes, I do," said Eleanor, closing up the back of the wagon, not telling him any more information as to her plans.

"Well, come inside, please. I have some meat scraps I'd like to send to the abbey. Mayhap you could use them to make something for the orphans."

"Thank you, that is very kind of you," said Eleanor, following him into his shop. "Tom, where is Finnian? I had hoped to pay him a visit while I'm here."

"I wish I knew," said Tom, putting down the bushel of apples and walking behind the counter to pack up some meat scraps for her. "He keeps disappearing. I'm afraid he might be out stealing again, though he denies it."

"Where is your wife?" Eleanor looked around the shop. It was very quiet. Usually, Tom's wife Alice always worked with him.

"She's at the church. Praying for Finnian. She does that a lot lately." Tom shook his head, seeming as if something was really bothering him.

"What's the matter, Tom? You seem troubled."

"I am," he admitted, using brown paper to wrap up the meat. "Finnian's actions have caused trouble between me and my wife."

"How so?" she asked curiously.

"I'm afraid that in anger, I accused Alice of being the problem. I told her she should be watching over the boy better."

"I'm sure it's not her fault. It isn't anyone's fault."

"I realize that, but the damage is done. Plus, I've had other vendors coming to me telling me Finnian has stolen from them."

"Is it true?"

"I'm afraid so. I recently found a pair of shoes in his room that we didn't buy him. And often I find bottles that smell like whisky."

"What do you tell the other vendors?"

"I can't admit the boy is a thief. It would ruin my business. I told Alice we need to send Finnian out on his own, but she won't hear of it."

"I'm sorry he is being such a problem. I thought once he had a family, he'd stop his stealing. This is my fault."

"Nay, Lady Eleanor. Don't say that." He handed her the package of meat. "My wife and I haven't been blessed with children, and when Finnian came to live with us, we thought our prayers had been answered. But now, instead, it seems as if it is naught but some kind of curse."

"I'll talk to the boy. Mayhap I can help him see that he is hurting you and Alice."

Just then, the door to the butcher's shop opened and in walked Finnian.

"Lady Eleanor." The boy stopped in his tracks.

"Hello, Finnian," she said with a smile. "My, you've grown since the last time I saw you."

"Where were you, boy?" growled Tom. "There is work to be done."

"You don't own me. Quit telling me what to do." Finnian hurried toward the back of the shop, but stopped when something fell to the floor from under his tunic.

"What's that?" asked Tom.

"It's mine," said Finnian, reaching for the pouch, but his father got to it first. He opened it and pulled out one shilling. "You were out thieving again, admit it."

"What do you even care?"

"Whose pouch is this?"

"Excuse me, but may I see that?" asked Eleanor, approaching them.

Tom gave her the pouch with the shilling, and she could see that the ties were cut. "I think I know whose this is," she told them. "Finnian, why did you steal this?"

"It's just from that bloody hangman, so what does it matter?" the boy bit off. "If I had known he only had a damned shilling, I wouldn't have bothered."

"I will beat you for this," snapped Tom, grabbing the boy by the tunic. Eleanor could see the fear in Finnian's eyes.

"Wait, Tom," she told the butcher. "I've seen the hangman in town. If I have Finnian give him back his pouch and money, will you promise not to hit him, but forgive him instead?"

"That's not easy to do. The boy is nothing but trouble."

"We can get through this together," she told Tom. "Please, give him a chance to change."

"Fine," grunted Tom, releasing the boy. "But the next time he steals, he will get the beating he deserves."

"Come along with me, Finnian," said Eleanor, handing the

pouch with the coin back to him. "We'll find the executioner and you can give it back and apologize."

"Me? Nay!" cried the boy. "He'll hang me or chop off my head."

"You should have thought of that before you decided to steal from him," said Tom.

"I promise you, nothing like that will happen. Now come," said Eleanor, holding out her hand.

"I don't want to go," protested Finnian.

"Lady Eleanor, do you think this is a wise idea?" asked Tom. "You are a lady. You shouldn't purposely seek out the hangman."

"I'm not worried in the least. It was I who brought Finnian to you, and I will be the one to make sure he returns what he stole and apologizes as well."

"Well, go on then, Finnian," said Tom with a jerk of his head. "Lady Eleanor doesn't have all day."

Finnian begrudgingly followed her out to the wagon, and they both climbed aboard.

"Why are you making me do this?" asked Finnian.

"Why are you turning into a thief, and it sounds like a drunk as well?"

"I'm thirteen. I can do what I want."

"I promised the butcher and his wife a boy to help them out. Now, you need to change your ways before you ruin everything for them, as well as for yourself."

CONNOR WAITED at the edge of town for Eleanor, his stomach growling from hunger. He cursed the fact he wasn't able to get food for his family. He also cursed his stupidity for not realizing a boy was stealing what little money he had.

The wagon pulled up, and Connor became even angrier when he saw that same thief riding along with Eleanor.

"You!" he shouted, darting out of the shadows. "You will pay for stealing from me."

"Lady Eleanor, help me," cried the boy, scooting closer to her on the bench seat. "That's the executioner and he is going to kill me."

"Connor, calm down," said Eleanor as she and the boy climbed out of the wagon. "Finnian is here to talk to you. Go on, Finnian."

"Talk? I have nothing to say to the swine. I ought to string him up for—"

"Connor, please. Give him a chance."

"You know the hangman by name?" asked the boy, making Connor realize this could cause trouble for Eleanor.

"Everyone knows my name," Connor told the boy. "I once used to be a nobleman, you realize."

"You were?" That seemed to surprise the little thief. It also seemed to bring some kind of respect between them. "Here is your pouch and coin," he told Connor, holding it out, but being careful to keep his distance.

"Is there something else you'd like to say to him, Finnian?" asked Eleanor.

"I'm sorry," said the boy. "I didn't know you were once a noble."

"Hrmph," grunted Connor, taking the pouch and looking inside to make sure the coin was still in there. "You shouldn't steal from anyone, no matter if they are noble or a commoner or even a hangman. Don't do it again. No good can ever come from it."

"What difference does it make?" asked the boy, sounding defiant.

"You know," said Connor, using the frayed string to tie the

pouch back on his belt. "I just came from the hanging of a thief. He wasn't that much older than you."

"Y-you did?" Finnian's hand went to his throat.

"That's what happens to thieves. They go to the gallows," he said, purposely trying to scare the boy straight.

"I returned your pouch. Now leave me alone." The boy turned and ran back down the street to the butcher's shop, running inside and slamming the door behind him.

"Connor, was that necessary?" asked Eleanor, raising a brow.

"Well, hopefully it'll scare him straight so he never steals again."

"I honestly think there are better ways to help the boy than that."

Thunder rumbled overhead and the sun was blocked out totally from the sky.

"We need to get going. It's about to storm." He reached out and helped her up to the seat of the wagon, liking the way her small waist and curvy hips felt in his hands. Then he climbed up after her and took the reins, driving the cart out of town.

"Since Finnian stole your money, I guess you never got food for your family?" she asked.

"Nay," he answered. "I guess I'll have to hunt when I get back."

"I thought you said it wasn't allowed. Not for another month."

"That's right."

"Well, isn't that dangerous?"

"Of course it is. So is starving to death," he told her, just as his stomach rumbled. He was not able to look at her when he said it.

She reached over the back of the wagon and then held out

an apple to him. "Here. Eat this. It'll help your stomach to stop rumbling."

"Nay. I'll take it back to my siblings instead," he told her.

"Connor, I saved an entire bushel of apples to give to you for your family."

"You did?" He turned a little to look at her.

"Yes."

"Nay. I don't need charity," he told her, feeling what little noble pride he had left rising to the surface.

"We have more apples than we can possibly use at the abbey, so you will be doing me a favor by taking them."

He looked over to her, wanting to kiss her right now. "Thank you," he said, under his breath. "It will mean a lot to my siblings."

"I also want to give you this." She slid a package wrapped in brown paper and tied up with string onto his lap.

"What's that?" he asked.

"Tom, the butcher gives me meat scraps to make stew and soup for the orphans."

"I won't take food out of the mouths of orphans."

"The only orphans left at the abbey are Lena and Margaret who are two and four years old. They don't eat much. Besides, neither of them even like meat. So take it. Please."

"All right," he finally agreed, nodding, feeling so choked up that he could barely speak. Damn it, he felt so pathetic and worthless. At one time he had promised to take care of Eleanor. To be her provider as soon as they were married. My, how the tides had changed. Now she was the one taking care of him instead. This is not the way things were supposed to be.

It started to rain just as they reached the outskirts of the abbey.

"I'll get out here so no one sees me riding with you."

Connor climbed out, sticking the package of meat under his arm.

"Don't forget the apples," she told him.

"Thank you. Again." He took the bushel of apples as well.

"Now you'll have to walk home in the rain. Won't you let me give you a ride?"

"Nay. It's not safe for you to travel alone. Besides, I don't want you getting wet. It's bad enough that your shoe is already ruined with mud." He turned to leave, carrying the bushel of apples.

"Connor, wait," she called out, causing him to turn around.

"What is it?" he asked her.

"I-I'm sorry for saying all those horrible things about you at the hanging. I know you really didn't want to kill that man, but had to do it."

"I told you, Eleanor, I didn't kill that thief. If it were up to me, I would have stopped the hanging altogether. My father wants me to start executing the prisoners, but I refuse to do so. He trapped my hand under his and pulled the lever."

"Oh, I see." Her hazel eyes looked wet, and it wasn't from the rain this time. She blinked away a tear. "So you haven't killed anyone? Not yet?"

"Nay," he told her. "But I do assist with the executions, but only to make it easier on my father. However, that might all change soon. My father is sick and I believe he is dying."

"It's not too late," said Eleanor. "Let me talk to my father. He has connections with the King. Mayhap he can get you out of this horrible position."

"Nay, don't even mention you saw or talked with me—it'll only mean trouble for you, Eleanor. That is the last thing I want."

"I'm not afraid of trouble. I want to do this to help you."

"It's too late, sweetheart. My fate was sealed the day my father took the deal, and there is nothing anyone can do to change the fact that I will be the next hangman, whether I like it or not."

CHAPTER 5

"I love apple pie," said little Alaric the next morning, sitting at the table holding one in front of him with his eyes wide. A smile crossed the boy's face and his tongue shot out to lick his lips.

"I know it won't be as good as Francesca used to make, but I think I remembered the recipe correctly, and had just enough flour and butter to make it," said Connor, having awoken before the others to make the special treat. Since they didn't have an oven, but just an open fire to cook over, he had cooked the shell of the pie first, and then added the apples so the shell would not get gooey. He cooked it all in a clay pot with a lid over it.

"I could have helped you. You should have woken me up," said his sister Ginevra with a yawn, sitting down at the table with a blanket wrapped around her.

"Nay, I wanted to let all of you sleep," Connor told them. "Besides, you made the stew last night.

"I still say you should have let me set traps in the forest to catch our food instead of taking scraps of meat meant for dogs," complained Leoric. "We don't need charity."

"Nay, Connor's right," said their father, emerging from the bedroom with his hand on his head. After all he had drunk yesterday, Connor was surprised he'd managed to get up long enough last night to eat stew with them. "It's too risky hunting when it isn't allowed," said Wensel. "I won't let anything happen to any of you." He sat down in his chair, sniffing the aroma that filled the air from the apple pie. "Damn, that smells just like the pie that your mother used to love," he told his children. "The cook at the castle would make it especially for her."

"It's not the same," said Connor. "I didn't have currants or honey to sweeten it, but the apples themselves weren't that tart. I used some dried mint we harvested last fall to give it extra flavor."

"It's delicious, Father," said Alaric, talking with his mouth full. "Try some."

"Yes, Father. There is plenty for all of us," said Ginevra, pushing the plate over to him.

"Nay," said their father with a shake of his head. "You eat it, sweetheart."

"Connor has more cooking. I'll wait," offered the girl, her eyes fastened to the pastry.

"There is enough for all of us. I made sure of that," said Connor, removing a pan with more from the fire, uncovering the shallow clay pot and placing it on the table. "There are even enough apples left to last us the rest of the week if we use them sparingly."

"So, Connor. You never told me where you got the meat scraps as well as the apples," said Wensel in a deep voice. "I hope to hell you didn't have to beg for the food. I don't want my children ever having to beg."

"Nay, Father," said Connor, knowing his answer would

upset the man, but also realizing he had to tell him. "It was a gift. From... from Eleanor."

His father's head snapped upward and his brows dipped. "Eleanor Blackmore?" he asked. "The girl you were once supposed to marry?"

"Yes, that's her," said Connor. "I saw her at the hanging and then again later on the road."

"Why are you even talking to the girl? It's over between you, Connor. *Over*. Do you hear me? We don't need anything from the Blackmore family. Leave them alone." His father jumped up so quickly that he lost his balance and started to fall. Connor was near him and rushed over to catch him.

"Sit down before you fall over," Connor told him, as his father started to have a coughing spell. "You need to regain your strength."

"His face is red," Ginevra pointed out.

Connor at first thought his father's face was flush from all the whisky he'd been drinking. But when he touched his father's forehead, his skin felt like it was on fire.

"You're burning up with fever," said Connor. "And your body is shaking like a leaf. You need to get back to bed immediately."

"I can't. I have work to do," Wensel protested.

"What work, Father?" asked Leoric. "Do you have to do another execution?"

"Nay," Connor answered for him. "There are no more executions planned for now. Not that I know of."

"I have to take care of my family," said Wensel, his eyes starting to drift closed.

"Leoric, take Father back to bed," Connor commanded, trading places with his brother and rushing to the hook on the wall for his cloak.

"Are you going somewhere, Connor?" asked Ginevra.

"Are you getting more apples?" asked Alaric, eyeing up the rest of the pie.

"Nay, I'm going to find a healer or some medicine to help Father," Connor answered.

"Where will you find that?" scoffed Leoric. "No healer will come here and you know it."

"I'll be fine," said their father, coughing even more.

"I'm taking the horse. It'll be faster. I'll do whatever I have to do to help you, Father," said Connor, hurrying to the door. "Ginevra, pat down his body with a wet cloth to keep him cool. Leoric, watch over your siblings as well as our father. You're in charge until I return.

"What about me?" Five-year-old Alaric, ran over and tugged on Connor's cloak. "What should I do?"

"You watch over the pie," said Connor, using his hand to ruffle the little boy's hair.

Connor left the cottage, knowing there was only one person who would be willing to help an executioner and his family. Then again, he wasn't sure getting Eleanor involved with his family and their problems was really the right thing to do.

"ELEANOR, YOU HAVE VISITORS," Sister Barbara informed her, as Eleanor headed across the courtyard to the refectory the next morning, holding the hands of the little orphan girls, taking them for something to eat.

"Me? Who would be calling here for me?" asked Eleanor in surprise. She stopped and turned to face her good friend. "Is it a man or a woman?" she asked, suddenly wondering if Connor had called on her for some reason. Part of her almost wished he had, but another part of her feared the idea. After all, it could only mean trouble for both of them if he showed up here at the abbey.

"Your cousins, Lady Raven and Lady Lark, are at the gate," announced Sister Barbara.

"Really?" Eleanor's worried frown turned up into a smile. "Sister Barbara, will you take Margaret and Lena to the refectory for something to eat while I greet my cousins?"

"Of course," said the nun, taking the girls and heading in the opposite direction.

Eleanor hurried to the front gate to find Raven and Lark, as well as one of the castle's guards just inside the entrance of the abbey.

"Raven! Lark!" called out Eleanor, picking up the hem of her skirt and running to greet her cousins. "What are you two doing here?"

"We came for a visit," said Raven. "I hope you don't mind."

Raven was a few years older than Eleanor and had a twin brother, Rook, as well as two younger brothers, Tolin and Daegel. Raven had long black hair and silver eyes. She was a lady who knew how to handle a weapon and wasn't afraid to use one. She was the daughter of Lord Corbett Blake, the brother of Eleanor's mother, Lady Echo.

"Mind? Of course not," said Eleanor. "I love seeing both of you. You two can stay in the guest quarters, as well as your guard."

"Oh, the guard is going back to the castle," said Raven. "We're going to be here for a while and I didn't want to impose upon him."

"Stay here for a while?" Eleanor became extremely suspicious.

"Aye, we thought ye might like a little company, or someone to talk to right now," said her Scottish cousin, Lark. Lark was the same age as Raven, but was half Scottish, being the daughter of the famous laird, Storm MacKeefe, who married Wren, the sister of Echo and Corbett. She had long blonde hair and green eyes, and was the mother of a little girl named Florie. She had a brother named Hawke and a sister called Heather back in Scotland.

"Really. You just got married, Lark," said Eleanor. "And Raven, you were complaining about not having enough time with your new husband. Yet, here you two are without your husbands, telling me you're going to be here for a while? With me?"

"That's right," said Lark with a smile.

"Uh huh," said Eleanor, crossing her arms over her chest. "Spill your secret. I know something else is really going on. Now tell me, what is it and why are you really here?"

"Och, all right," said Lark, being the first to break. "We heard from one of the guards at the castle that ye were seen talkin' with Connor right after the hangin'."

"Lark!" scolded Raven. "You weren't supposed to say that."

"Well, she asked," said Lark with a shrug. "I only answered honestly."

"You never could keep a secret, could you?" scoffed Raven.

"I'm fine. Really," said Eleanor. "You two don't need to worry about me."

"So, ye really did see the executioner, then? The man ye were goin' to marry at one time?" asked Lark curiously.

Eleanor looked around, seeing that they were creating a stir and some of the nuns were close enough to hear their conversation. She didn't need this information being part of tomorrow's gossip.

"I think we should go somewhere else to talk about this," said Eleanor. "Tell your guard to go get something to eat. I'll get my horse and we can take a ride to the orchard by ourselves."

It wasn't long before the three women were in the orchard just outside the abbey walls. Eleanor dismounted, tying the reins of the horse to a tree, and plucking an apple, giving it to the horse. Lark and Raven did the same for theirs.

"It's such a beautiful, sunny day," said Eleanor, finding a patch of grass that looked halfway clean and plopping down on the ground, lying back with her eyes closed and her face to the sun. "Have a seat," she told the others.

"Go on, Lark," said Raven. "I'll stay standing and keep watch."

"I dinna want to sit on the ground in my good gown," protested Lark.

"Have it your way," said Eleanor, soaking in the sun.

"Ye ken, we are nobles and shouldna be out in the sun at all," Lark reminded her.

"By the rood, Lark, you're from the Highlands and live in a hut in the mountains most of the time," said Raven. "How did you get to be so finicky?"

"Sorry. I guess being at the castle has changed me." Lark fluffed out her skirt and sat down on the ground next to Eleanor.

"As nobles, there are a lot of things we shouldn't be doing, and I don't really care," Eleanor replied.

"Like meeting in private with executioners?" asked Raven.

Suddenly, the mood changed. Eleanor sat up and faced her cousins. "Is that why you two are here? To try to convince me to stay away from Connor?"

"We didna say that." Lark looked the other way.

"It's true, isn't it?" Eleanor stood up and brushed off her gown.

"Cousin, my father heard you've seen the hangman, and he is concerned that you will somehow shame the family name," admitted Raven. "He sent us here to make sure that doesn't happen."

"Hah! Now, that is amusing," said Eleanor. "Uncle Corbett is forgetting that my mother—his own sister—was once a pirate. That didn't seem to worry him, so why would anything I could possibly do concern him?"

"He's afraid ye'll marry Connor, now that ye have been speakin' with him again," said Lark.

"Lark, you didn't need to tell her that much," said Raven from the side of her mouth.

"Connor has been through a lot in his life. Bad things happened to him that he didn't deserve," Eleanor told them. "I feel bad for him."

"He's an executioner now," said Lark. "Ye need to stay away from him, Eleanor, Uncle Corbett is right. The hangman is dangerous."

"Nay, that's not true," Eleanor told them. "It's Connor's father doing the executing. Connor hasn't killed anyone."

"Mayhap not yet," said Raven. "However, it's his fate to become an executioner and he has no choice. He will execute people sooner or later."

"Connor was my best friend and I miss him dearly. Remember, we were once betrothed," Eleanor reminded them.

"Yes, but things changed. That was a long time ago." Raven put her hand on Eleanor's shoulder. "Why don't you come back to Blake Castle with us for a while? It'll help you to forget about Connor, as is proper."

"Nay!" Eleanor pushed Raven's hand off her shoulder. "I don't want to forget about him. Ever. Besides, I still have two orphans to look after at the abbey, so I can't leave."

"Ye can bring the orphans with ye. I'm sure Uncle Corbett willna mind," suggested Lark.

"I don't know," said Eleanor with a shake of her head.

"Connor's family is struggling and going hungry. That is why I helped him by giving him meat scraps and a bushel of apples. But that won't last long. They need more. He needs me."

"There is a man comin' towards us," said Lark, jumping up and shading her eyes from the sun.

"Who is it?" Raven's hand went to the hilt of her sword.

Eleanor turned to see the undeniable silhouette of Connor as he climbed the hill to the orchard. His head was covered by his cloak, but she had no doubt it was he.

"Connor," she said in a mere whisper.

"It's Connor?" asked Lark, still trying to see through the sun.

"He's here? What does he think he's doing?" Raven started to draw her sword, but Eleanor raised her hand to stop her cousin.

"Please, Raven. No. He's not here to harm us, I promise."

"Then what does he want?" asked Lark, sounding suddenly nervous. "We shouldna be seen with an executioner. He shouldna be here at all."

"I know that, and so does he," said Eleanor. "Something must be wrong if he's come here. Let me talk to him alone."

"I'm not leaving you. I'm going to protect you," said Raven in her stubborn way.

"Me too," said Lark, her hand going to her waist belt that held her dagger.

"Nay. Stay here. Both of you. And please, don't embarrass me," instructed Eleanor. "I'm going to talk to him. Alone."

She ran to meet him, stopping as she got closer, watching as he lowered his hood to make his identity known.

"Eleanor. I'm sorry to bother you here," said Connor. "I hope I'm not causing trouble."

"Connor, you shouldn't be coming here. Someone might see us."

"I see your cousins, Lark and Raven are with you. Hello," he called out, nodding toward the girls. Lark crossed her arms over her chest and Raven turned to let him see she had her hand on the hilt of her sword. Neither of them returned his greeting.

"I told them to stay there," Eleanor explained. "Don't worry, they won't say anything. I'll make sure of it."

"I shouldn't have come," he said, putting his hood over his head again. "I'll leave. I don't want to be a burden."

"Wait," she said, as he turned around to go. "Is something wrong?"

He paused for a minute and she didn't think he was going to tell her. Then he let out a deep sigh before answering. "It's my father. He's ill and grows weaker every day."

"Is his sickness contagious?" asked Eleanor.

"I don't think so," Connor answered. "I believe if it were, my siblings and I would have been infected already. He's had a cough for a long time and wheezes. He drinks until he collapses, and now he's got a raging fever."

"Oh no! You need a healer," said Eleanor.

"Aye," he answered.

"But I'm not a healer. Why did you come to the abbey?"

"I-I'm not sure. I guess I was hoping that one of the monks or nuns might... it was silly. What was I thinking? No one will come near an executioner. My mistake."

"You're right that no one will help an executioner," said Eleanor. "No healer, anyway. But my cousin Rook's wife is a gardener and knows a lot about herbs. Mayhap Rose could give me something that would help to heal your father."

"Nay. It's too risky for you to even ask," said Connor, shaking his head. "If anyone found out."

"They won't," said Eleanor, taking his hand. "Come with me." She pulled him up the hill, back to Lark and Raven.

"Eleanor? What are ye doin'?" asked Lark, taking a step back, as if she were afraid to stand too close to Connor.

"You shouldn't be bringing him up here," warned Raven. "No good can come of this."

"Connor needs our help," said Eleanor. "His father is dying."

"We canna do anythin'," said Lark. "Why ask us?"

"Lark is right," agreed Raven. "Don't get involved, Eleanor."

"I told you this was a bad idea," said Connor, looking as if he'd just lost all hope.

"Nay! I think Rose might know of some herbs that could possibly cure his father's fever or help his cough," Eleanor explained to her cousins.

"Mayhap, but Rose isna here," said Lark.

"We need to send for her. We can't just let Connor's father die." Eleanor felt that this was the right thing to do, no matter how much her cousins might object to the idea.

"Eleanor, if he is that sick, no amount of herbs will be able to save him," said Raven, her fingers finally releasing the hilt of her sword.

"If his father dies, Connor becomes the next executioner," Eleanor reminded her cousins. "God's eyes, we can't let that happen!"

"You're right," Raven finally agreed. "I will send the castle guard to Rookrose Manor with a missive for Rose, telling her she is needed and to come anon."

"Make sure Rook doesn't find out about why we want Rose," said Eleanor. "If he knows what we're doing, he won't let his wife come here."

"Aye, Rook is a stickler for following rules, unfortunately," said Raven.

"He married a gardener and you think he follows the

rules?" asked Connor, with a slight chuckle. "I tend to see things differently, I guess."

"You need to send the guard at once," said Eleanor. "It'll take nearly a day to get back to Devon, and another to return here. There is no telling how long Connor's father has to live."

"Are you sure there is nothing that anyone here at the abbey can do to help him?" asked Connor. "Anything at all?"

"I wish there were," said Eleanor. "If it were under different circumstances—"

"I understand," said Connor. "You don't even want to ask, and I can't blame you a bit. Thank you for any help you can give me. And also for the meat scraps and apples," Connor said, looking directly at Eleanor. "It meant a lot to my siblings. Alaric is in love with apple pie."

Eleanor looked around, and saw an empty bushel basket lying on the ground. "While you're here, let's pick some more apples for your family," she suggested. "Everyone is in the refectory eating right now, so we won't have to worry about being seen."

"We'll go find the guard and give him a missive for Rose at once," said Raven. "Come on, Lark."

"Is it safe to leave her alone with him?" asked Lark behind her hand.

"I heard that, and I assure you, I will not hurt her. I will protect Eleanor with my life," Connor promised.

"Go on," said Eleanor, with a wave of her hand. "I'll be safe. Don't worry."

Once the girls left, Eleanor picked up the empty basket. "I think that tree looks like it has a good amount of ripe apples." She led the way and Connor followed.

. . .

CONNOR once again felt as if he were putting Eleanor in an awkward position, and was already starting to regret coming here at all.

"Are you sure Lark and Raven won't say anything about all this? I don't want to cause trouble for you."

"If they do, they know they'll have hell to pay with me," said Eleanor with a smile.

"I've never known you to be so feisty."

"A lot has changed over the past five years, Connor. I'm not that same shy girl you once knew."

"I am starting to get that impression. Here, let me carry the basket." He reached for the basket, and his hand brushed against hers. When it did, she stopped walking, her eyes looking up at him. The sunshine made her red hair look brighter and her hazel eyes even clearer than he ever remembered them being. "God, you are beautiful." He couldn't help himself from reaching out and cupping her cheek. Instead of pulling away from him like anyone would do if someone like him came close, she leaned into the caress and closed her eyes, welcoming his touch.

"Connor, that feels so good," she cooed.

Connor felt such an attraction to this beautiful woman that he couldn't stop himself from leaning in closer. "I hope you'll think this feels just as good," he whispered, just before pressing his lips up against hers. He had only meant it to be a quick kiss, but when her hands came up to his chest, and instead of pushing him away, she slid her hands up to his shoulders and pulled him closer, he decided to go back for a second helping.

This kiss was even better than the first, since she participated now. Eleanor's lips melded with his, holding all the passion of a lover. His heart beat rapidly in his chest, and for one moment in his mind, he was a knight. Her lover. Her betrothed. Then the sound of swords and creaking ropes filled his mind and he was reminded of the cruel reality of exactly who he was now. He jerked away from her, his hand going to the raised burn mark on his cheek that told the world he was an executioner.

"I-I'm sorry," he said softly, feeling as if he had no right to kiss a noblewoman. Not anymore. "I just got caught up in the moment."

"Don't be sorry. I liked it and wanted it just as much as you did." A wide smile spread across her face.

"I have wanted to kiss you for what seems like forever, Eleanor. But now that I did, I know it's not right. We shouldn't have kissed at all."

"Don't say that," she told him. "It's not right that we are no longer betrothed."

"Nothing can happen because of this."

"All we're doing is picking apples. Now stop all the worrying and help me get that red one right up there. It's too high for me to reach it." She looked over at him playfully. "Will you pick me up?"

"I know what you're doing, Eleanor. It'll only prolong the agony for both of us."

"Just shut up and pick up me so I can reach the apple."

That actually made him laugh aloud. "I guess you really have changed. The Eleanor I remember never would tell a man to shut up."

"The Eleanor you remember is gone and the new one is more determined than ever to get back the man she's always loved, and lost."

"Loved? Do you mean that?"

"I do," she told him. "I think these years apart have only made me realize how much I really care for you. I wish we could be married, like we were once supposed to be."

"I know what you mean," said Connor. "I think about it every damned day." The wind blew a stray strand of her hair across her face, and he boldly reached out and tucked it behind her ear. Then he kissed her once more, wrapping his hands around her waist and picking her up high over his head.

She squealed and laughed, holding on to his broad shoulders.

"Pick the apple. It's right over your head," he told her. "I promise I won't drop you."

She did pick the apple, and when he put her down their eyes interlocked. Connor felt like that young boy again, for a moment in his life all his troubles dissolving when Eleanor smiled at him. He half expected her to start singing, taking his hand and running through the field. But of course, that was naught but a memory of the past, and it didn't happen. It would never happen again.

"You realize today has been our first kiss," she told him.

"I know," he answered, staring at her mouth. "You don't know how many times in the past I had thought about it and planned it. I think waiting all this time has only made the kiss even better than I had ever imagined it would be."

"Me too." She boldly kissed him again, then took a bite of the apple. Holding it up to his mouth, she offered it to him, and he took a bite as well.

"Eleanor, if things had worked out, we'd be married by now," he told her. "I'd be a knight and you'd be my wife. We might live in a manor house and even have our own orchard."

"And lots of babies."

"Yes," he said, swallowing hard, feeling his emotions welling up within him.

"I'd like that," she said. "And I will never give up hope that it will someday still happen."

"What the hell are we doing?" He shook his head and ran a hand through his hair.

"We're entitled to dream," she told him.

"Are we?" he asked. "Because somehow, I feel like it's wrong to dream. So very wrong."

"Let's not ruin the mood, Connor. Now, help me pick the apples so you can get them home to feed your family." She reached up and started picking apples from the tree.

"Why are you so good to me, Eleanor? Everyone else is repulsed by me and my family."

"I intend to treat you no differently than if you were a knight."

"Then you're in for a lot of disappointment, because I can no longer be your knight in shining armor, even if it's the only thing I really want in life right now. God's eyes, all I want to do is to protect you and care for you. Yet here you are, taking care of me instead."

"You have always watched over me, Connor. You know as well as I that if you hadn't saved me when I fell into the lake, I would have drowned."

"At least I taught you to swim, so something good came out of it." He smiled and squeezed her hand in his.

"It'll take a few days for the guard to get the missive to Rose and for her to return," said Eleanor as they filled the bushel with apples. "In the meantime, I am going to make sure that your father and your entire family have enough food to eat. Mayhap some chicken soup will help your father's condition. I can bring some over."

"You don't even know where I live," he told her.

"Nay, but I bet I can find it if I tried."

"I don't want you coming into the woods looking for me, Eleanor. The creek has been flooding lately from all the rain and it's too slippery and dangerous."

"Ah, so you live by the creek in the woods, that tells me."

"I don't want you seeking me out. You might step on one of the snares I use to hunt."

"And you're in Lord Sampson's woods hunting so that means I know exactly where to find you."

"Eleanor," he said, looking at her from the sides of his eyes as he filled up the basket. "Promise me you won't try to find my home."

"The new Eleanor is inquisitive and doesn't make promises she doesn't intend to keep."

"Well, the new Connor isn't as carefree as the old one. This one is warning you to stay away from me and my family if you know what is good for you."

"Oh, I see Raven and Lark down by the abbey gate with the guard. You'd better go now, so the guard doesn't see you. Hurry."

"Thank you," said Connor, picking up the bushel of apples and boldly kissing her once more on the mouth. "For everything."

With that, he turned and left, wondering if kissing Eleanor hadn't been the best decision after all. Or the fact that they professed their love for each other.

After all, nothing could ever come of it.

She was a noblewoman.

He was an executioner.

And if there is one thing he knew about the lives of nobles it was that they were not allowed to marry anyone from below the salt.

CHAPTER 6

"What were ye and Connor doin' up on the hill yesterday?" Lark asked Eleanor the next morning. "Ye never told us."

The two girls were staying in the guest house of the abbey that was used for travelers. Now, however, they were all in Eleanor's room, since she had overslept and they came to wake her.

"We were picking apples," said Eleanor with a yawn, having had a good night's sleep. She'd been dreaming of kissing Connor and didn't want to get up. "What do you think we were doing?"

Eleanor quickly dressed, knowing that Sister Barbara and the orphans would be waiting for her down in the courtyard. She had promised to take the girls to town today if the weather was nice. They were also going to visit Hamlin and Bertram again as well, since the girls said they wanted to play with their dog.

"We thought you were kissing," said Raven. "Or at least that is what it looked like to me."

"Oh!" Eleanor pulled the gown over her head and fixed her bodice. "We were," she admitted. "Your guard didn't see us, did he?"

"Nay. Lark kept him occupied looking at her since the guard seems to like her."

"Remember, I'm married now, Raven. I dinna think Dustin would like to ken that ye told me to flirt with that man."

"It was for a good purpose, and to help Eleanor," said Raven. "We couldn't have the guard seeing her being so careless, could we?"

"I wasn't being careless." Eleanor sat down on a stool to put on her shoes.

"Well, what would you call kissing an executioner out in plain view?" asked Raven. "Even I knew if I wanted to kiss a commoner to do it in private."

"Me too!" said Lark.

"Well, Connor isn't a commoner. Or at least he didn't used to be." Eleanor stood up and brushed the wrinkles out of her gown.

"Sit down and I'll braid yer hair," said Lark, pushing Eleanor back down on the stool as she started to braid.

"So, what shall we do today?" asked Raven.

"Anything that doesn't consist of trying to talk me out of liking Connor," mumbled Eleanor.

"I dinna ken how ye can like an executioner."

"I was mean to him at the hanging, like everyone else. But then I realized that there is still hope," said Eleanor. "Connor is not a bad man. He doesn't deserve what has happened to him."

"What does that mean?" Raven sat on the bed polishing her sword with a rag.

"It means, I thought he was the one doing the executions, when he was only assisting."

"What is the difference?" Lark finished the braid and tied a ribbon around the end. "Either way, he is still executin' people."

"Not really. He is not directly responsible for killing innocent people."

"I wouldn't call the people being executed *innocent*," said Raven.

"Mayhap not, but don't you see? Connor doesn't yet have that sin on his soul."

"Sin on his soul?" asked Lark. "Och, Cousin, are ye sure ye are no' really a nun after all?"

"I am far from being a nun, because even when I thought Connor had executed him, I couldn't let him go. He has been in my heart so long that it doesn't feel right to just abandon him. He needs me. I know that now."

"I say we start our day and forget about all of this for now." Raven put away the rag and got to her feet, pushing her sword into the scabbard hanging from her waist belt.

"I'm taking Lena and Margaret to visit the boys today, and we're stopping in town. Do you two want to join me?"

"Why no'? I promised Florie I'd bring her a present when I return," said Lark. "Mayhap we can find a shop that sells somethin' little girls would like."

Lark's husband was once her four-year-old daughter's tutor, and also the castle scribe. Florie was sired by another man, but Dustin was now her father.

"Why didn't you bring Florie with you?" asked Eleanor. "She would have liked playing with Margaret and Lena."

"I suppose that would have been a good idea. Mayhap they can still meet someday."

"If I'm out with the children I usually take an escort, but since you are here, Raven, we won't need one. Let's go." Eleanor headed for the door. "I want to put a few bushels of pears into the back of the wagon before we leave."

After visiting at the farm of Mr. and Mrs. Woods, Margaret and Lena were having so much fun playing with the boys and the dog that they didn't want to leave.

"Come along girls, we have another stop to make in town yet," said Eleanor.

"Can't we stay here a little longer?" asked Margaret.

"Please?" begged little Lena, hugging the dog. "I want to throw the ball for Roger. I didn't get my turn yet."

"We want the girls to stay, too," said Bertram. "We missed them."

The orphans were like siblings, and Eleanor felt bad making them leave since they wanted to stay together.

"Why don't you go to town and come back later for the girls?" asked Edna, holding a bowl of warm pears she had just taken from the fire. "I am going to serve these pears over a slice of fresh rye bread. I think the children will enjoy it." She made the treat from the bushel of pears Eleanor gave the family. "Albert is finishing up the chores for the day, and he'd like to see the children playing together too, I'm sure."

"Well, I suppose that would be all right," said Eleanor. "I will return soon with my cousins. Thank you, Edna. And tell Albert thanks as well."

The women got back on the front seat of the wagon and headed for town. They had just entered the outskirts of town when they spotted some sort of commotion up ahead. A small congregation of people were huddled out in front of the cordwainer's shop. There was a lot of shouting and swearing going on. It seemed like trouble was at hand.

"I think we'd better go," said Lark. "It looks like trouble brewin'."

"Mayhap it would be a good idea to leave," agreed Raven. "We can come back at a later time."

Eleanor was about to agree when she heard someone

mention the name Finnian. Then she saw Tom, the butcher, in the center of the crowd waving his hands in the air.

"They're talking about Finnian," said Eleanor.

"Who?" asked Lark.

"Finnian was one of my orphans. I think something must have happened. We'd better go find out what is going on," Eleanor told the others. "I can't leave until I know."

They had just approached the group as everyone left, going their own ways.

"Tom, Tom!" called out Eleanor, making her way toward the man.

"Lady Eleanor? What are you doing here?" asked the butcher.

"I was coming to buy a few things for the abbey when I heard the commotion. What is going on?"

"Oh, there have been a few more thefts in town and everyone is accusing Finnian of being the thief."

"Oh, no," said Eleanor. "Did Finnian do it?"

Tom looked one way and then the other before answering softly. "I'm afraid it's true. I found a few of the stolen items in his room. I returned them and even bribed the owners with free meat, begging them not to say anything. I'm giving away more than I'm selling lately, I swear. Eleanor, I think it was a mistake for my wife and me to take in Finnian. All he's been is trouble."

"Tom, these are my cousins, Lark and Raven," said Eleanor, introducing the other women.

"Ladies," said the butcher, with a nod and a slight bow. "Town is nowhere for unescorted noblewomen to loiter."

"Don't worry. I have my sword and know how to use it if we encounter any trouble," Raven told him.

"Finnian is the twelve-year-old orphan that Tom and his wife took in a few years ago," explained Eleanor.

"He's thirteen now," Tom corrected her. "Yesterday was his birthday. We couldn't afford to give him a present, and I think that is what caused the boy to go out and steal items from the townsfolk. He just took whatever he wanted and has no remorse for his actions."

"Oh, I am so sorry about that," said Eleanor. "I feel bad since I have been so distracted that I forgot it was the boy's birthday. This is partially my fault, I fear."

"Can you find him a new home?" asked Tom. "You would be doing me a favor."

"You really don't want him anymore?" Eleanor's heart broke for the orphan. Everyone needed to be wanted, no matter how much trouble they were.

"We like having him as our son, but honestly, I don't think Finnian is happy with us," Tom told her. "My wife refuses to give him up, but I'm afraid if we keep him any longer, I'm going to get run out of town or go broke and put out of business, trying to bribe the other shop owners to stay quiet about Finnian's little problem."

"Where is Finnian now?" asked Eleanor.

"God only knows where that boy is. I can't keep track of him and run a business too."

"I'm sorry for all the problems, Tom. I will look into finding Finnian a new home as soon as I can. In the meantime, I'd like to purchase a chicken from you."

"You would?" Tom made a face. "Doesn't the abbey have their own chickens?"

"Well, yes. But most of them are egg-layers and I need one that we can eat."

"All right. Come to the shop and I'll get one wrapped up for you right away. God knows I can use the sale."

Once the man walked away, Raven grabbed Eleanor by the arm. "Why are you buying a chicken? The abbey has enough of their own, and I know for a fact they aren't all egg-layers."

"I know. But this one is for someone else. Plus, I want to try to support Tom after all the trouble he is having with Finnian. I don't want him to lose his business."

"Oh, look at that rag doll in the window at the tailor's shop," said Lark. "I think that would be a nice present for Florie. I'm going to go buy the doll for her."

"Raven, can you pick up some scented beeswax candles as well as some honey and a bar of soap from the chandler's shop while I go get the chicken?" Eleanor dug into her pouch and handed her cousin a few coins.

"Are you going to tell me what this is all about?" asked Raven.

"Later. Now, hurry. I have one more stop to make before we pick up the girls."

CHAPTER 7

Connor returned to the cottage with Leoric, having caught nothing in the snares they'd set up in the woods. They'd also had to hide from Lord Sampson's guards, who were patrolling the area. This wasn't good. His father had used most of their money on whisky lately. Between that, and the fact that Connor would always pay off a lord at an execution so the dead wouldn't be displayed, and Connor constantly giving the widows of the executed their coin back, it had put a strain on his family.

They entered the house to find their father at the table, barely able to hold up his head. In his hand was a wooden cup of whisky.

"Where were you two?" growled his father.

"We were checking the traps in the woods," said Leoric.

"Dammit," spat Wensel, swigging down the last of his whisky and throwing the cup across the room. "I told you not to risk it. One of you is going to end up in prison if Sampson's guards catch you."

"And if we don't hunt, we're all going to starve," yelled

Leoric, storming back to the door. "I'm going to hunt, no matter if it kills me."

"Nay!" said Connor. "You'll stay here with Father and your siblings."

Ginevra and Alaric sat quietly at the other side of the room.

"Connor, Father is just a drunk and you know it," spat Leoric. "Why don't you do something about this? We can't go on living this way."

"Stop it," said Connor in a soft voice.

"Nay, I won't stay quiet about this any longer," said Leoric. "Father has doomed us all by his poor decisions." He looked back at his father. "I wish you would have died that day instead of taking the position of hangman and ruining all of our lives forever." Leoric left the cottage, slamming the door behind him. Connor's father got up and stumbled to the bedroom, slamming the door behind him as well.

"Connor, what are we doing to do?" cried Ginevra.

Alaric ran to him and threw his arms around him. "I'm scared," said the little boy.

"Don't be," Connor answered. "Everything will work out."

"How can it?" said Ginevra, crying now. "We have no money and we're going to starve to death."

"I assure you, I won't let that happen—now calm down. Tomorrow I will go with Leoric to Marvane Castle to clean the garderobes. We'll have money soon."

"Marvane Castle?" asked his sister. "That's where Mother died. I miss her, Connor. And I miss Francesca, too."

"I know. So do I," he answered.

Alaric tugged on his tunic.

"What is it, Alaric?" asked Connor, seeing his little brother staring up at him with wide, innocent eyes. "Are you going to shovel poop?" he asked. "That's icky."

"I'll do whatever it takes to provide for my family. Now,

why don't you two go visit Francesca's grave. But don't wander into the woods. And if you see Leoric out there, tell him to stay close to the house as well."

"Will you come with us?" asked Ginevra.

"Nay. I'm going to talk to Father. Now go."

His siblings left the house, and Connor walked over to the bedroom, not at all sure what he was going to say to his father. He raised his fist and knocked quickly, then entered the room. His father sat on the edge of the bed with his head in his hands.

"Can we talk?" Connor asked him.

"There is nothing to say," the man mumbled, staring at the ground. "Leoric hates me and he has every right to. I can't blame him."

"He doesn't mean it." Connor walked into the room, sitting on a chair across from his father.

"I should have died that day. He's right. I have ruined the lives of all of my children."

"No one blames you for the situation we're in."

"You do, don't you?"

Connor didn't say a word. He had blamed his father, as well as himself. But saying that right now wasn't going to help the situation.

"I drank away all our money, and now my children are going hungry."

"I'll take Leoric with me tomorrow to Marvane and we'll clean out the gong pits," said Connor.

His father's head shot up. "Nay!" he growled. "Isn't it bad enough that we kill people? I won't let my sons shovel the shit of the man who made me this way."

"Father, your own doings put you in this situation and you know it. In case you're forgetting, you killed Lord Sampson's brother."

"How can I forget?" His father lowered his head again shaking it back and forth. "But honestly, I would do it all over again, because I was protecting the name of your mother."

"What's done is done," said Connor. "But you've got to stop drinking so much. It only puts more stress on the family."

"Do you know why I drink so much?" asked Wensel. "It's because I cannot accept the fact that I'm an executioner."

"I understand."

"Do you? Do you really?" His father got up and started to pace the floor. "I have nightmares each night that are so terrifying I wake up in a cold sweat. I see the faces of those I've killed and they are all out to get me. So, before each execution I get drunk so I don't have to realize what I'm even doing. Afterwards, I punish myself for what I did. I don't like to see the widows crying for their husbands' lives that I was responsible for taking. It pains me to see the children of the deceased crying for their dead fathers. So I punish myself and drink so I cannot feel that pain."

"What do you mean?"

"Look," said his father, pulling up his tunic, showing Connor the welts on his back and on the front of him too. Some of the wounds looked to be infected.

"God's eyes, what did you do to yourself?" Connor jumped up and went over to inspect the wounds.

"This is what I do," said his father, opening a drawer and pulling out a whip. "I whip myself for my sins. I punish myself not only for taking the lives of the prisoners, but also for ruining the lives of my own children, when all I wanted to do was to protect you."

"Father," said Connor, not able to believe what he was seeing and hearing. "I had no idea."

"Of course not. I always did it away from you and your siblings so you wouldn't know and try to stop me. I would have taken my own life long before now but didn't. Because if I did, I knew you'd have to fulfill the role of hangman, and I didn't want to do that to you, Son. You deserve so much better than this stinking life."

"Then why have you been trying to convince me to pull the lever and do the executions?" asked Connor.

"Because, I am dying and we both know it. I only do that because I want you prepared when the day comes. I'm sorry that it has to come to this." His father's knees gave out and he fell to the floor.

"Father!" cried Connor, running to him, and picking him up in his arms. He carried him to the bed and laid him upon it. "You are still burning up with fever."

"Let me die, Connor. My wounds are deeply infected and I can feel it eating away at me. There is nothing you can do to stop my death, and no healer will ever step foot into our cottage to even try to help me."

"Nay, that's not true," said Connor. "I have sent for Rose, the wife of Lord Rook Blake. She is a gardener and will know how to use herbs to heal you. She should be here any day now. Just hold on. Help is on the way."

"You did what?" he asked, and grimaced. "Nay, don't get the Blake family involved. And stay away from Eleanor. It will only bring you both heartbreak."

Before Connor had a chance to answer, the door to the bedroom swung open and Leoric stuck his head inside.

"Connor, come quickly," he said.

"Not now, Leoric," growled Connor. "Now leave us alone. I will be there shortly."

"But someone is here to see you."

"What?" He spun around to look at his brother. No one ever came to their cottage. In the entire time they'd lived in the woods, no visitors ever came to call, because of who Connor and his family were now. "What are you saying? Who is it?"

"Connor, it's me," said Eleanor, poking her head into the room. "I am here with my cousins, Ladies Raven and Lark. We have brought you something."

"Bid the devil, Eleanor, how did you find me?"

"I talked to the undertaker who told me where you lived."

"Well, turn around and leave quickly before anyone sees you here." Connor swished his hands in the air, trying to get her to go.

"Nay, I won't," she answered stubbornly.

"Dammit, Eleanor, you shouldn't be here, and you know it. Now go."

"I brought some things for you and your family. They are in the wagon. Please don't send me away."

"Father, get some rest," said Connor. "I'll be back shortly." He covered his father with a light blanket and guided his brother and Eleanor from the room. "What is this all about?" he asked Eleanor.

"Please don't be angry that I'm here."

"Well, I'm not happy about it. This is no place for you or your cousins. I told you not to come."

"She has food for us," said Leoric. "Don't send her away."

"How is your father?" asked Eleanor.

"He's been better. Let's talk outside so he can get some rest."

As soon as they made their way outdoors, he saw his younger brother and sister talking with Lady Raven and Lady Lark. They stood next to the wagon.

"What did you bring us?" asked little Alaric. "More apples for pie?"

"Well, I think we'll let Lady Eleanor tell you," said Raven, as Eleanor and Connor approached the back of the wagon. There were some things in the back covered by a blanket. The cart was also filled with hay.

"I hope you like what I brought," said Eleanor.

Connor noticed the blanket moving. "I think someone is hiding in the wagon." He hopped up on the back, reaching underneath the hay and pulling out a boy by the front of his tunic.

"You!" shouted Connor. "Trying to steal from me again?"

"FINNIAN!" gasped Eleanor, surprised to see the boy hiding in her wagon. She'd had no idea he was there.

"Don't hurt me, hangman. I was just trying to sneak out of town." Finnian held a pear in his hand, with a bite taken out of it.

"Your father is looking for you, Finnian," said Eleanor. "He and your mother are very worried."

"No, they aren't. I heard Tom tell you that he wished he never took me in, and I heard you say that you were going to try to find another family for me," said the boy.

Well, there was no hiding the truth now, since he already knew. Still, Eleanor didn't feel comfortable speaking about this right now.

"Connor, please, let him go," said Eleanor.

"Why should I?" asked Connor. "This boy is nothing but trouble."

"Nay, he's not. He's a good boy, just confused, and not sure how to behave," protested Eleanor, feeling attached to each and every orphan that she'd cared for and placed in homes.

"Were you stealing again?" Connor asked the boy, but Finnian didn't answer. Next, he looked over to Eleanor. "Was he?" She couldn't lie to him. If she did and he found out, he'd never speak to her again.

"Yes, he did. From several townspeople and they are not happy," she reported.

"They blame everything on me, even if I didn't do it," cried Finnian. He still looked very scared.

"That's because, I'll bet, most of the time you're responsible for the crimes," Connor ground out.

"Finnian, go home," said Eleanor.

"They don't want me there," said the boy stubbornly. "I'm going to live in the woods from now on. Or maybe here?" He flashed a quick smile, still holding the pear.

"Like hell you are," Connor responded, finally releasing the boy. "I have enough mouths to feed and don't need another one."

"I can help bring you food," said Finnian, taking another bite of the fruit.

"I don't want stolen food." Connor didn't sound like he was going to budge with his decision.

"Mayhap it would be better if Finnian stayed here with you until things cooled down in town," suggested Eleanor. "At least, no one would ever come here to look for him."

"Over my dead body." Connor stretched out his arm and pointed in the direction of the road. "Go back home and take the punishment you deserve. Once and for all, you are not staying here."

"Fine," said Finnian, finishing off the pear and throwing the core over the side of the wagon. He hopped down and brushed the hay off his clothes. "I'll go back, because even if no one likes me there, they still like you even less." With that, he turned and ran from the cottage toward the road.

"Eleanor, we really should get back and collect the girls,"

said Raven. "It's not fair to leave them with the Woods family this long."

"Aye," agreed Lark. "Besides, I canna wait to show Florie what I got her." She pulled the rag doll out from under the hay and picked off a few strands.

"What's that?" asked Ginevra, coming closer to see it. Her big eyes devoured the doll as she looked at it with longing.

"This is a doll for my daughter," said Lark.

"She is a beautiful doll." Ginevra's eyes were fastened to it. "I had a doll my mother made me when I was a child, but it's gone now."

"Ginevra, you're eleven. You're too old for dolls," said Leoric with a roll of his eyes. "Can I have a pear?"

"Sure," Eleanor answered. "Can you take the bushel of pears into the house?"

"I sure can." The boy jumped up on the back of the wagon to get it.

"I want to help," said Alaric, trying to get up there but being too short to do it.

"Here you go, Alaric." Connor reached down and pulled the little boy up atop the wagon by one arm. Then, he hopped down and brushed his hands together. "The pears look good, but you really shouldn't have done that, Eleanor."

"Why not? Your family needs to eat," said Eleanor. "I brought you another gift as well." She reached over and picked up the chicken and held it out. "This is to make chicken soup. It'll be good for your father."

"Chicken soup?" Leoric licked his lips. "I can't wait."

"Ginevra, do you think you can make chicken soup?" asked Connor, taking the bird and handing it to his sister. Her eyes were still fastened to the doll in Lark's grasp.

"Yes. Yes, I can do that."

"Then go. Both of you," said Connor, sending Leoric and Ginevra into the cottage. Alaric sat on the end of the wagon kicking his feet back and forth.

"Here are a few other things." Raven handed Connor the bag from the chandler's shop next.

Connor curiously looked inside. "Beeswax candles? We live in a hut of wattle and daub, not a church. These are only for the rich and the clergy."

"I know. But I thought the scented candles would be a special treat for you," said Eleanor. "To help ease all the stress your family is going through."

"Since soap doesn't ease stress, I am guessing you are saying I smell bad and need to wash?" Connor held up the soap and raised a brow.

"Nay. Not at all," said Eleanor, feeling suddenly embarrassed since that wasn't her intent.

"Show him the rest." Lark reached over to the wagon and held up a big corked jar of honey. "This should go good when you're making the pies."

"I see." Connor took the jar, staring at it, not able to say the words *thank you*, but neither did Eleanor care. She just felt good to be helping out his family.

"I suppose we'd better go now," said Eleanor. "I don't want to impose on Mr. and Mrs. Woods by leaving the girls there too long."

"Goodbye," said Lark, walking over and getting onto the front seat of the wagon.

"Enjoy the food," said Raven, seeming lost for words and a little uncomfortable being there at all. She joined Lark in the wagon.

Connor looked over at Eleanor, and she couldn't help seeing the sadness in his eyes. He also seemed as if his pride was hurt by what she had done, even though he didn't admit it. Then again, he didn't give the things back either.

"I'll pay you for all of this as soon as I get a side job and earn some money," he told her.

"Nay. There's no need for that. It's a gift."

"Dammit, Eleanor, I don't want gifts! I will provide for my siblings as well as my ailing father on my own."

"Oh? And how will you do that? Do you have another execution planned soon?"

"Well, nay. But I will find another way to earn the money."

"Doing what?" asked Eleanor, knowing damned well that no one would ever hire an executioner for anything. Or at least not for any decent job.

"I was going to go to Marvane Castle to clean the gong pits, but my father doesn't want me to go. He feels it is too belittling to our family after what Lord Sampson has put us through."

"I agree," said Eleanor. "Surely there is another way to earn coin."

"Does the abbey's gong pit need cleaning?" he asked, surprising her since she didn't expect him to say that.

Eleanor felt like crying. Just thinking of Connor doing such a demeaning job made her feel ill. She couldn't even bring herself to answer.

"Well? Does it?" he persisted, making her want to cry now. She knew he wouldn't stop asking until he received an answer, and part of her wouldn't let her lie.

Slowly, she nodded.

"Good. Then tell your abbess that my brother and I will be there first thing in the morning to clean it out."

"Connor, I can't let you do a job like that."

"It's not any worse than hanging a man or lopping off his head, is it?"

"Well... no, but still..."

"Don't say another word about it. It doesn't matter."

"Yes, it does matter. Connor, you are—"

"Shhhh," he said, holding his finger up to her lips. She felt the warmth of his skin against her and it felt damned good. "I'd rather we didn't speak of what I am."

"I was going to say—" She had meant to tell him he was too good to do a demeaning job like that, but he stopped her once again.

"You'd better go. Your cousins, as well as the Woods family, are waiting. Come on, Alaric." Connor grabbed his little brother by one arm and lifted him up, then set him on the ground. Alaric held out his hands.

"I want to carry the honey."

"All right, but be careful not to drop it." He gave the jar to Alaric. The little boy took it and sprinted toward the house.

"Hold it with two hands, and slow down," Connor called out after his brother.

God, Eleanor wanted to reach out and kiss him right now. Still, she didn't think Connor would want her to do that. It wasn't the right time or place. She'd just hurt his pride and she didn't want to push it or embarrass him any further.

"You'd make a good father," she said softly so her cousins wouldn't hear her.

"Well, we'll never know since I will never get married."

"Nay? Why not?" she asked curiously. "You used to tell me you wanted five or six sons."

"At one time I did," he answered, hanging his head. "But now, I don't want any children."

"Why not?" she asked in surprise.

"Eleanor, everything has changed," he told her. "I once wanted to be a knight like my father. I wished for sons to be knights like me. I always wanted my children to follow in my footsteps. But not anymore."

"Oh," she said, realizing exactly what he meant.

"Thank you for your thoughtfulness, but please, this needs to stop. And I don't ever want to see your face at my door again."

He turned and walked away, leaving her standing there feeling alone, empty... and severely broken-hearted.

CHAPTER 8

"Eleanor? Aren't you coming to break the fast?" Raven stood in Eleanor's doorway with Lark the next morning, waiting for her to join them.

"I'm not hungry." Eleanor stared out the window, watching Connor taking his cart to the back of the abbey where the garderobes emptied from the abbey out into an open area down below a hole in the floor. His brother Leoric was with him.

"What are ye lookin' at so intently?" Lark walked up next to her and gazed out the window. "Isna that Connor and his brother?"

"Where?" asked Raven, hurrying over to look out the window as well. "What is Connor doing here? And so early in the morning?"

"He's here to clean out the garderobes," said Eleanor, stepping back and closing the shutter. She just couldn't watch this anymore. "Shall we go?"

"Wait a minute," said Raven, looking at her inquisitively. "Why is Connor cleaning out garderobes?"

"It's the only type of job an executioner and his family can get," answered Eleanor sadly.

"Ye mean, besides executin' men," added Lark.

"Yes, that is what I meant, but I don't care to talk about it any longer." She took a step toward the door, but Raven grabbed her arm to stop her.

"This must be hard for you to see."

"It doesn't matter," Eleanor answered. "It is much harder for Connor to have to endure, yet he does it and does not complain. Now, let's go."

"Eleanor, this is horrible," said Lark. "Surely, there must be somethin' we can do to help him?"

"I already tried that by bringing food to his family," explained Eleanor, shaking her head. "In doing so, I believe I only managed to bruise his pride."

"Surely, that's not so." Raven released her arm.

"No?" she asked, looking up at her cousin. "He told me not to repeat the action, and that he never wants to see my face at his door again."

"I'm sure it's just for yer own safety," said Lark, trying to make her feel better, but it didn't.

"Nay, that's not it." Eleanor felt her emotions welling up inside her.

"Then what is it?" asked Lark.

"Connor has accepted that he will never be anything but a hangman. He has lost all hope that mayhap someday we can still end up together."

"Well, it does look that way, I'm sorry to say." Lark had a tendency to be blunt at times, and this was one of those times that Eleanor wished she hadn't.

"I'll never give up hope," said Eleanor. "I know we were meant to be together."

"Still, you can't put your own life on hold waiting for

someone and something that nobles are not allowed to have or do," Raven pointed out.

"I agree," said Lark. "Ye need to keep livin'. Forget about Connor and accept that ye must live on without him. It's the best thing to do."

"How can you two say such a thing?" Eleanor was aghast at the uncaring attitudes of her cousins. "Lark, you put your life on hold for five years, waiting for a man to return who had a wife and was never coming back for you."

"It's no' that," said Lark. "That's no' what happened." Lark seemed suddenly sad.

"Then what was it?" asked Eleanor.

"I was... undesirable, and no man wanted me. That is, no' until I met Dustin." Her eyes lit up again and a smile spread across her face.

"Dustin, the scribe," said Eleanor. "The man from below the salt that nobles are not allowed to marry."

Lark's smile faded.

Eleanor addressed Raven next. "And you, Raven, did everything in your power not to have to marry a noble that you didn't know or love."

"True," answered Raven. "But I found Jonathon, and a true love that I would have never known being naught but the prize of a competition."

"Jonathon Armstrong," said Eleanor. "A blacksmith. Another man from below the salt whom noblewomen are not allowed to marry."

"Jonathon is an armorer, not a blacksmith. Not really," said Raven, looking bothered by what Eleanor said. "Besides, he's a master armorer now, and is paid well and respected highly by the nobles."

"Dustin is the castle scribe and respected by the nobles as well," Lark was sure to get in.

"I know," said Eleanor with a deep sigh. "I didn't mean to sound snobby, I'm sorry. I like Dustin and Jonathon very much, and I am happy for both of you."

"Well, we like Connor, too," said Raven softly.

"I am in love with Connor," said Eleanor, looking down and wringing her hands together. "I'm not ready to give up hope that we can still be married someday. I know he's no longer a noble, but he used to be one. And you two married men who were never nobles until they gained their courtesy titles by marrying the two of you."

"So, ye think yer father as well as Uncle Corbett will allow ye to marry a hangman?" asked Lark.

Raven blew air from her mouth. "My father might have accepted an armorer and scribe into the family, but I assure you, he'll never welcome an executioner with open arms. It is unthinkable."

"I agree," said Lark. "And yer father, Eleanor, being Lord Warden of the Cinque Ports cannot allow it or the king would have his head."

"Then we need to figure out a way to change all this." Eleanor refused to let her cousins talk her out of it. She still wanted Connor, and she had to find a way to make that happen.

"Change what?" asked Raven. "Eleanor, I'm sorry, but you need to accept the fact that when Connor's father took the position of hangman to save his life, he also decided the future of his children. Especially Connor."

"That's true," agreed Lark. "They realized what they were gettin' into before they agreed to it. It was their choice, and now they must live by it."

"It was his father's choice, not his." Eleanor fought for Connor.

"Nay, Eleanor." Raven shook her head. "I'm sorry, but we

all know it was Connor who made the decision for his father that day."

"So, you're saying he purposely chose to give me up—to lose his wealth, his title, and his chance of being a knight and married to me? That it is was what he wanted?" She could feel her heart about beating out of her chest. She didn't want to believe this. It just couldn't be true.

"Aye, it was his decision," said Lark. "I'm sorry, Eleanor, but it's too late for ye and Connor to ever get back together."

"Nay!" shouted Eleanor, her hands balling up into fists. "I won't accept that. I don't believe it."

"Eleanor, please." Raven walked over and put her arm around Eleanor's shoulders. "There is nothing we can do. You just have to accept it."

Eleanor couldn't help it, and started crying. Lark walked over to hug her and comfort her.

"Ye ken we would go to the ends of the earth to help ye if we could," said Lark. "There is just no way out of this one."

"But I love him," said Eleanor, sniffling. "I will only love *him*, and never another man. Connor doesn't deserve this. It just isn't right."

The church bells started ringing, being heard clearly even with the shutter closed.

"Let's go pray for him, then," suggested Raven.

"I think that is a good idea." Lark walked over and opened the door. "If we canna help him, then mayhap God can."

"I'll pray for his soul, but I'm not sure Connor even believes there is a God anymore," said Eleanor, leaving the room with her cousins, not sure she believed either.

THE CHURCH BELLS RANG LOUDLY, filling Connor's head with silly thoughts like weddings. Marrying Eleanor to be exact. He jumped off the wagon, picking up a shovel from the back, feeling the eyes of every nun and monk burning into him, pitying him for the man he had become.

"Ugh, it stinks back here," said Leoric, making a face. Usually Connor and his father cleaned out the garderobes while Leoric hunted and tended to the other children. With his father being too ill to help him, Leoric had come in his place.

"You'll get used to it after a while," said Connor, removing a wheelbarrow from the back of the wagon as well. He then handed his brother a pair of knee-high boots, and donned some himself. They'd have to not only shovel up the sludge, but then haul it away and bury it in a vacant field. Some farmers used it as fertilizer, but Connor wasn't friends with any of the farmers, and wasn't willing to go door to door asking if they wanted to buy shit.

Most gong farmers just dumped it in the river or lake, but Connor refused to defile the waters in that manner. After all, that is where his family obtained their drinking water since they didn't have a well. It was also where they bathed. He waded out into the pit of sludge trying to ignore how demeaning this damned job was, or how bad it smelled.

"Isn't that Eleanor and her cousins?" Leoric stretched his neck, waving to the women as they headed across the walkway with the two orphan girls, heading for the church.

Connor looked up to see Eleanor wearing a bright blue gown. Her hair was braided and wrapped around each ear, and she wore a small veil on her head. Even from this distance, he could see her rosy cheeks and glowing disposition. She glided with grace over the stone walkway, while Connor stood knee-deep in smelly waste. He couldn't help thinking she probably smelled like roses right now, while he stank like—nay, he refused to acknowledge any of this. It would only make the job harder, as well as drive him mad.

"Don't wave to them, you fool," he growled at his brother, sinking the shovel into the cesspool. "Don't even look their way."

"My, you sound bitter," said Leoric, taking a few squishy steps into the cesspool, standing near Connor. He coughed and started to gag just from the smell. "God's feet, this stinks. I don't want to do this."

"Then leave. I can handle it alone," said Connor, not wanting to see his brother be as humiliated as he was right now. "Why don't you go home and watch after Father? I'm not sure Ginevra and Alaric should be with him alone if he's been drinking, which I'm sure he has."

"Nay, I should stay here and help you. Besides, Father says I need to start helping with the executions. I'm sure this isn't half as bad as that."

"You have no idea." Connor scooped the sludge into the wheelbarrow.

"I can do this," said Leoric, looking down at the cesspool, coughing and gagging again. This time he nearly vomited.

"Go!" commanded Connor, snatching the shovel out of his brother's hand and throwing it to the ground just outside of the cesspool. "I never should have let you come with me in the first place."

"Are you sure about this?" Leoric's face turned red and he bent over and retched.

"You are of no use to me if you can't even scoop a shovelful without gagging."

"Well, mayhap it would be a good idea after all if I'm there to watch after our siblings. I might check the rabbit snares on the way back and search for some wild parsnips or herbs we can use in the pottage."

"Fine. But you'll have to walk back since I need the horse and wagon to get this job done."

"It's all right. The walk in the sunshine and fresh air will do me good. Mayhap it'll help to calm my roiling stomach." Leoric eagerly hurried through the muck, removing his boots when he got back to the wagon.

"Be careful," called out Connor. "Don't let Sampson's guards see you. We have enough trouble as it is."

"I'll be careful, I promise. I'll blend right in to the woods, so don't worry." His brother left at a run, leaving Connor standing there by himself to do the disgusting work that a man with noble blood in his veins should never be doing.

He looked up to see Eleanor on the walkway overhead. The walkway led from the second-story bedchambers to the church. She was watching him, and it made him angry as well as humiliated. Their eyes interlocked. Then she raised her hand to wave at him, but stopped in midmotion. Her cousins came back and dragged her away.

Connor lowered his head, pulling at his hood harder, trying to cover as much of his face as possible. Then he dug his shovel into the sludge once more, trying to think of anything but his shame. Eleanor had just seen him at what had to be one of the lowest point of his life.

CHAPTER 9

Connor stripped off his clothes and dove into the water of the lake. It had been a long morning emptying the gong pit of the abbey, since he sent his brother home and had to do all the work by himself. After emptying and cleaning out his wagon, he now needed to wash his body too. Using the soap that Eleanor had brought him from the chandler shop, Connor had scrubbed the stench first from his clothes and boots, and then from his body and hair.

It was a warm day and he had worked up a sweat. It felt free and invigorating floating in the cool waters of the lake that was halfway between the abbey and his home. He broke through the water's surface with his eyes closed and his face raised to the sun. God's eyes, it felt good. For a moment he had almost forgotten all his troubles, feeling like a youth again. He used to always sneak away to the lake with his friends and loved lying on a rock in the sun, even though nobles weren't allowed to do such frivolous, carefree things. After saving Eleanor from almost drowning, he had been sure to teach her how to swim, holding her up so her head wouldn't go below the water. It felt good to help people. Or at least it used to. Now, all his worries were about helping his family and himself.

He emerged from the water, wringing out his long hair and walking back to the shore.

That's when he saw her.

Eleanor stood on the shore next to her horse, looking like the angel he always knew her to be.

"Eleanor," he said, frozen to the spot and unable to move.

"Hello, Connor." She shyly turned her head and looked the other way to avoid his nakedness, even though he wasn't at all embarrassed that she saw him in the nude. "I wanted to talk to you alone."

"All right," he said, his eyes flitting over to his clothes laid out in the sun on a rock to dry. He made his way back to his horse, where he had dry clothes stored in the travel bag. "Give me a minute to dress."

"Of course."

As he stepped into the dry trews, he glanced back over his shoulder, catching Eleanor watching him. It did his heart good. So, she was truly still interested in him after all.

"See anything you like?" He flashed a quick smile.

Her eyes opened wide and her head snapped around when she realized she'd been caught peeking at him. Once again, she looked in the opposite direction. "I don't know what you mean."

"It's all right. You can look now," he told her, leaving his chest bare and walking over to greet her.

"Oh!" she said, her eyes settling on his chest. He noticed her gaze dropping lower and lower, settling on his waist. "You are still not dressed."

"I'm wet and without a towel. I'll just go without a tunic until I dry off in the sun. Unless it bothers you?"

"Of course," she said, and cleared her throat. "I mean, nay. It doesn't bother me at all." Her cheeks looked flushed and she seemed to be talking in a gibberish manner, as if she couldn't think straight.

That pleased Connor for some reason. Mayhap it was only because he liked knowing that his nakedness affected her. That told him he was still desirable to a noblewoman. The only women who had ever seen him without clothes were whores. And they never blushed like a maiden when looking at his naked chest, the way Eleanor was doing right now.

"You shouldn't have come here by yourself. It's not safe on the road," he scolded her, worried for her safety. "How many times do I need to tell you to take an escort with you?"

"I'm not alone. I have an escort. Two of them, actually."

"You do?" He squinted in the sun, looking for a guard or a monk but didn't see anyone. "Where?"

"Raven is here with her sword, and Lark with her dagger. The both of them are waiting for me just around the bend behind the trees if I need them. But I won't. I know I am safe now that I am here with you." Her words were so sweet that they touched his heart.

"Oh." Now it was his turn to react the same way. He wondered if the other ladies had seen him naked as well. Either way, none of this really mattered, so he dismissed the thought from his head. "You said you wanted to speak to me?"

"Yes," she said, clearing her throat. "It seems the abbess accidentally underpaid you for the work you did cleaning out the gong pit. You left before she could stop you. I told her I'd bring it to you. Here you are." She held out a pouch that jingled with coins as it dangled between her long, elegant fingers.

"Truly, Eleanor?" He raised a brow, knowing she was lying. "The abbess paid the amount we agreed upon," he informed her. He knew what she was doing, although she might have thought she was being clever. "If you wanted to see me so badly, sweetheart, you should have come up with a better lie than that."

She made a face that told him his assumptions were true.

"All right, I admit I did want to see you again," she told him. "And the abbess didn't give me this money to bring to you, but it is something I personally wanted to do. It's money for your family. And to help your ailing father."

Anger grew within him. Connor didn't like a woman constantly providing for him. That was a man's job and she was belittling him by doing so. "I don't need or want your money," he spat. "Put it away and don't insult me again, because I don't like it." He walked back to his horse, attaching the steed back up to the wagon, since he had let the animal drink and eat grass while he bathed.

"Your pride is going to be the ruin of you yet, Connor. Let it go," she said, following him. "Please take the money." Once again, she held out the pouch. "Your father might need medicine."

"We won't know anything about my father's condition until your friend Rose shows up, and she still isn't here yet."

"I know. But I'm sure she will be here soon."

He did nothing to take her money, and couldn't even look at her right now. He busied himself preparing to leave.

ELEANOR SLOWLY LOWERED HER HAND, realizing once more she had managed to hurt Connor when all she'd intended to do was to help him.

"All right, then," she said, attaching the money pouch to her belt. "If you won't take the money, then at least join me for something to eat."

"Indeed," he said in a sarcastic tone. "And where would we dine?" he asked, fastening the harness to the horse as he looked back up the road. "The abbey? Do you really think the abbess is going to invite an executioner to sup with her at her holy table?"

"The abbey is a safe haven for all those who travel and even accepts orphans left on the doorstep," she told him.

"Aye, but do they accept the reapers of death as well? I sincerely doubt it."

"Don't call yourself that."

"Why not? After all, that is the way everyone sees me now, so why pretend it isn't true?"

"Stop it!" she said, becoming angry with the way he was acting. "I hate it when you talk like that."

"Well, what did you expect me to do? Offer to bring the wine? Or how about saying, I will pick a bouquet of flowers for you, too, that we can place on the table? You make this sound as if we are courting, for God's sake, when it is the furthest thing from the truth."

Eleanor wanted to cry when he said that, because actual courting was the exact thing they had never had the opportunity to do. They were ripped apart before any real romance could have bloomed. It was also what she craved the most between them.

"You need to stop feeling sorry for yourself, Connor. Instead, be thankful that someone like me still cares enough for you to even ask you to eat with me in the first place."

"So, I should be thankful now, should I? Grateful for my life as a hangman? Is that what you're saying?" She could tell his anger was bottled up inside him. He'd never stop torturing himself in this manner.

"No, of course not. That's not what I meant." She lowered

her head. "I just wanted to spend time with you. I feel as if we were harshly torn apart much too soon, when we were always meant to be together."

"That's in the past. It's all over now, sweetheart. That was naught but a dream crushed under the heel of the devil, and there is nothing we can do to get it back. Now, you'd best be on your way before someone sees you talking with me."

"I don't care who sees us! Can't you understand that?" A wave of emotion ripped through her. It had been exciting to see him naked. Even now, she couldn't stop staring at his naked chest and arms, wondering how it would feel to be pressed up close to him. He had developed into a man now, and she was a woman with needs. She needed his arms around her. She wanted his lips caressing hers. But none of this was ever going to happen when Connor could do nothing but pity himself and the way his life turned out.

"What I can't understand is why you keep pursuing me," said Connor. "Go live your life, Eleanor. Forget all about me because you are only hurting yourself with this girlish infatuation. It's over between us. And for God's sake stop following me around because it's only making this whole damned thing harder on both of us."

"Is that really what you want? For me to leave and never see you again?" Connor was shunning and dismissing her and she didn't like it one bit. Everything about their situation made her feel sad. "All I wanted to do was to meet with you in private so we could talk and be alone together. Can't you even allow me that?"

"If we do, it will only bring trouble."

"You don't know that! Besides, what difference does it even make? Can't we at least enjoy what little time we have together?"

He let out a deep sigh, looking as if he had given up all hope, even if she hadn't.

"I don't know," he mumbled, shaking his head.

"Please, Connor. Please, don't turn me away." She walked up to him and laid her hand on his arm. His eyes followed.

"You deserve someone better than me, Eleanor. Just forget about me and find a nobleman to marry."

"I don't want anyone but you."

"If you won't change that silly thought, then, you'll end up being a nun after all and we both know it. We can never be together. Not ever."

"Meet me at the home of Mr. and Mrs. Woods tomorrow morning. I'm going to bring the girls there for the day. I'll be able to slip away for a few hours."

"Eleanor, don't put me in this position. There is nowhere for us to go. Nowhere that a hangman and a noblewoman could be that wouldn't cause tongues to wag and eyebrows to raise. It'll only put you in danger."

"Nay, it won't. I swear it. Mayhap we can sneak off to the woods where no one will see us."

"It's not a good idea. Sampson's got guards patrolling the woods at all hours."

"If you are going to push me away like this, at least allow me one day with you. A few hours. Time when we can be alone and talk. Just like we used to when we were young. When we were betrothed and supposed to be married."

"Even if I do show up, this will change nothing between us, Eleanor."

"Just be there," she said, looking up, seeing Raven and Lark riding toward them. She reached up and kissed him on the mouth, and then rushed back to her horse. "See you tomorrow, bright and early," she said, as she mounted her steed.

"I'll think about it," was all he said, but it was music to her ears. At least he didn't outright say *no*. This gave her hope. Hope that she and Connor could be together again, even if it was only for a day or for an hour. Now, all she had to do was to come up with a way to save Connor from his awful life, because as he said, they could never end up together if he continued to be a hangman.

CHAPTER 10

"You're up early." Connor's father emerged from the house to join Connor, who was sitting at a stump cleaning two rabbits at the break of day. "Is something bothering you, Connor?"

"Good morning, Father. How are you feeling?" He didn't even look up, but just kept cleaning the rabbits.

"It hasn't been a month yet. You shouldn't be hunting. Sampson's guards are going to see you and arrest you." His father seemed severely out of breath. He sank down, almost collapsing atop a wooden bench, resting his elbows on the wooden table Connor had built. During the summer, on nice days, his family ate together outdoors.

"We have to eat, Father. I checked the traps early before the guards show up, and I wasn't spotted. These two rabbits should be enough for Ginevra to make stew. I also brought more root vegetables from the cellar." One of the first things they'd built after the house, was a small cellar out back. It was underground and cool and they used it to store meat and vegetables.

"Leoric should be cleaning those," grumbled Wensel. "He needs to learn."

"He knows how to do it, but has a weak stomach." Connor put down the knife, holding up the skinned rabbit to check it. "Leoric retched at the gong pits and couldn't even handle that. I had to send him home."

"I told you, I don't like you cleaning gong pits."

"It was at the abbey, not Sampson's castle. We need the money, Father. I had to do it."

"Well, I want Leoric to start joining us at the executions from now on. If he can't skin a rabbit or clean out a gong pit without being squeamish and retching, how is he ever going to handle a hanging or a beheading?"

Connor put down the rabbit, wishing his father would stop insisting Leoric do these things. The boy wasn't cut out for it. "Nay, Father. It's not a good idea."

"Of course it is. Your brother has told me himself that he wants to learn the trade."

"Trade?" Connor's head snapped up. "Is that what we're calling it now? Because I don't see taking lives as a trade at all."

"You know what I mean." His father groaned and struggled to breathe.

"I'll assist you at the executions, but leave Leoric out of this."

"When I die and you become the hangman, Leoric will need to assist you. The boy needs to learn."

"I said *no!*" Connor jumped up, feeling his anger growing within him once again. God's eyes, he never used to get this angry when he was a page or a squire, training to be a knight. What was the matter with him? "It's nothing he can handle and I don't want to put him through it."

"God's eyes, Connor. The boy is sixteen. He's a man now. Yet, you coddle him like he's a sister instead of a brother."

"I just want what is best for my siblings. That's all."

"I feel dizzy, Son. I think I'll go back in and lie down for a bit." His father got up, staggering and almost falling.

"Father!" Connor jumped up and put his arm around him. "You still have a fever," he said, feeling his forehead. "Let me get you something to drink, made from herbs. Mayhap that will help."

"Nay, I'll be fine," he said, coughing, waving a dismissing hand through the air. "I just need to lie down, that's all. I'll feel better soon."

Connor helped his father into the house. "As soon as I finish with the rabbits, I'm going to take a walk to town," he informed him.

"To town? Whatever for?" asked his father.

"I just need to get out and think for a bit."

"Take the horse and wagon."

"Nay. I might be gone a long while. I'll leave the horse and wagon in case you need it since you are ill."

"I'm not going anywhere today. Take it, I say."

"I'd rather walk," said Connor, not wanting anyone to notice the executioner's wagon when he met up with Eleanor today at the home of Mr. and Mrs. Woods.

"ELEANOR, face it, he's not coming," said Raven as the morning went on and they visited at the home of Albert and Edna. The children ran around playing while Roger, the dog, chased them, barking. Albert was turning over the small garden next to the house, and Edna was weaving a basket out of willow rods, or withies, that had been collected last year.

"I agree," said Lark. "Connor is no' goin' to show up here, no matter how badly ye wish it."

"Shhh," said Eleanor, noticing Edna glancing over at them. "I don't want Edna or Albert to know I asked Connor to their home."

"Albert, we need to harvest the peas before it rains," Edna called out to her husband, glancing up at the darkening sky. "You can finish turning over the garden later."

It was Sunday and the only day that the serfs were allowed to have a break from their work for the lord of the castle. This was usually the time when the serfs tended to their own personal gardens and repairs to their homes, or took care of other needs.

"I'm going as fast as I can," called out Albert. "If the boys helped me, it would go faster." He headed over to a heavy plow that was hoisted up on blocks that he'd been repairing. Taking off his hat, he leaned on the plow, taking a break.

"They will help you, dear," Edna called back. "Later. But they miss their sisters and are having so much fun playing together right now."

Albert grumbled some more and then he yelled out and started cursing.

"Albert!" Edna threw down the basket and ran over to the garden.

"Something is wrong," said Raven. "Let's go see if we can help."

Eleanor started to follow her cousins, but stopped when she saw a tall man in a hooded cloak stop on the road. She squinted her eyes in the sun, trying to see who it was. Then the man slowly lowered his hood.

"Connor," said Eleanor in a breathy whisper.

"Eleanor, are ye comin'?" asked Lark, looking back at her.

"Lark, it's him. Connor came. Go on without me." She turned and ran to the road to greet him.

"Good morning," said Connor, still just standing there, not moving.

"Hello, Connor. I'm so glad you came." Eleanor nervously played with the cross hanging on a chain around her neck. "I wasn't sure you would."

"Neither was I," he answered.

"Eleanor, come quickly!" yelled Lark, waving her down. "Albert is hurt."

"What?" she whirled around to see Edna over by her husband. Her hands were flailing around in the air. Albert was on the ground under a heavy plow. He was moaning and calling out. Even the children ran over with the dog to see if they could help him.

"He's trapped under the plow," cried Lark.

"Let's go," said Connor.

"Nay. You'd better not make your presence known," said Eleanor. "Just wait here."

"Like hell if I'm going to do that," growled Connor. "I can see from here that heavy plow fell on the man. The women aren't going to be able to move it and neither are the children. Now, get out of my way because he needs my help."

Connor took off at a run and Eleanor had no choice but to let him go. She ran after him, stopping when she saw Albert under the plow with his leg trapped.

"The damned thing fell on me," screamed Albert. "I feel like my foot is crushed."

Edna and Raven pulled at the plow, trying to right it, but it was heavy and wouldn't budge.

"Out of the way." Connor ripped off his cloak and threw it to the side.

"Good God, it's the executioner," shouted Albert. "Stay away from me. Don't touch me." His eyes opened wide in fear. "I don't want to die."

"I'm not here to take your life, you fool," said Connor. "I'm here to help you. Now, everyone get back. And keep the children and the dog out from under my feet."

"I don't want your help. I don't need it," protested Albert, still wanting nothing to do with a hangman.

"Please, Albert," begged Eleanor. "Let him help you. Connor is my friend. He means well. Don't be afraid of him."

"Yes, let him help you, Albert," cried his wife.

Eleanor grabbed the hands of the girls, while Raven kept the dog away and Lark took the boys out of danger as well. They all watched as Connor reached down and took ahold of the plow. His face turned red and his muscles bulged as he lifted the plow off Albert. "Fast, move your leg," said Connor.

"I- I can't move it," cried Albert.

"We'll help." Eleanor shot forward, and with Raven's help they pulled the man away and Connor slowly let the plow back down.

"Let me see your leg, you old fool." Edna got down to inspect it.

"Is it broken?" asked Lark.

"Nay, it's all right," said Edna, feeling her husband's leg. "I think he's just twisted it, that's all. Albert, you're going to have some nasty bruises."

"I see blood!" shouted little Hamlin.

"Let me see." Eleanor got down on her knees in the dirt, pulling back one of the legs of Albert's trews. "It is a scratch that is bleeding, but it's not deep," reported Eleanor. "I am sure I can wrap it up and it'll heal on its own."

"That blade was on his leg," said Edna. "In another minute, it could have dropped further and cut off his leg. Thank you, Connor, for helping him. If you hadn't been here, it would have been so much worse."

"Yes, thank you," said Albert, clearing his throat. "You were a big help."

"Let's get you in the house and clean you up," said Edna.

"I'll help him," said Connor, helping the man to stand, bringing him to the house. The others followed. "You need to sit down and rest, Albert, or that leg will never heal."

"I can't rest. I have to get the garden turned over and the peas need to be harvested before it rains. Plus, I've got to kill a chicken for dinner."

"Albert, you will not be able to dig with a shovel for at least a few days or mayhap a week." Edna brought a rag and water over to clean his wound. "What are we going to do?"

"I can help you," said Connor, causing them all to look up. "I'll have the garden turned over in less than an hour. Just put a shovel in my hand and watch what I can do."

Eleanor had seen him with a shovel at the gong pits. Even though Connor was born of noble blood, he could outwork any commoner. Plus, he was as strong as an ox.

"Nay. Nay, we can't ask you to do that," said Albert, raising his hand and shaking his head.

"Why not?" asked Eleanor. "You need the help. And I can take the boys and harvest the peas before the rain comes."

"Yes. We can all help," said Raven.

"Nay. You are nobles," said Edna. "This work is below you." Her gaze roamed over to Connor.

"I agree the women shouldn't do the work," said Connor. "However, I'm not a noble. Not anymore, that is. I'm willing to help you, unless you are embarrassed to have me here because of who I am."

"Nay, we are not embarrassed," said Edna. "Are we Albert?"

When Albert seemed as if he wasn't going to agree, Edna elbowed him in the side.

"Nay, we're not embarrassed to have you here. It's fine, if

you want to finish digging up the garden," said Albert. "I need to transplant the winter crops I started, and I am already behind schedule."

"I want to help you dig the garden too," said seven-year-old Bertram, seeming anxious to do it.

"Why not," said Connor. "Sure, you can help me."

"There are extra shovels in the barn," Albert told them.

"I want to pick peas," said Hamlin.

"No, no. I will do it when I am finished cleaning Albert's wound," said Edna.

"Edna, the boys were brought here to help with our chores," said Albert. "Let him do it. They've got to learn sooner or later."

"I agree," Eleanor spoke up. "We will all harvest the peas and I won't hear another word about it."

"Yes, we will," said Raven. "If we hurry, it'll be done before it rains. Lark, will you help us?"

"I- I—yes, of course," said Lark, not sounding as anxious to do it as the rest of them, but still she didn't say no.

Edna had tears in her eyes. "Thank you. Thank you all so much. I feel so blessed to have such wonderful friends as all of you."

Eleanor looked up to see Connor slipping out of the house so she followed.

"Connor," she said, as they got out to the barn. "Thank you."

He picked up a shovel and started digging up the ground. "Eleanor, I don't mind helping them. They are good people. But you and your cousins shouldn't be doing the work of peasants. It's not right."

"Let me decide what I want or don't want to do," she told him. "Right now, I feel this is the right thing to do."

"You always were stubborn, sweetheart."

146

"And you were always there when you were needed, Connor. Just like now."

He stopped and looked up at her, and she smiled.

He smiled back, but it was a sad smile. Still, he had showed up today, and now the Woods accepted him and that made Eleanor happy. Hopefully soon, more things would be changing for the better in Connor's life.

CHAPTER 11

A lbert had decided he wanted to go out and help harvest peas with the others, even if he had to sit on the back of a wagon to do it. So, they all left for the field, but Eleanor decided to stay back with Connor after all. Little Bertram had been helping to dig in the garden, but Eleanor sent him along with the rest of the children and adults to harvest peas instead, wanting to be alone with Connor.

"I would pick up a shovel and help you to dig if I didn't think you'd stop me," said Eleanor.

"You even *try* it and I swear I'll tackle you, bringing you to the ground." Connor thrust the end of the shovel into the dirt and reached up to remove his tunic.

"Y-you're taking off your tunic?" she asked, staring at his naked chest once again, not able to look at anything else. He had muscles and strong forearms and a taut stomach. Little dark curls of hair splattered his chest, leading downward and disappearing under the waist of his trews. He looked so good and so sexy that Eleanor had to stop herself from running to him and rubbing her hands against him.

"I'm hot," he told her, continuing to dig. "Why? Did you want me to put my tunic back on?" He looked back at her with hooded eyes that warmed her to the core. Did he look dark and dangerous, or was it just her imagination? She liked it. This mysterious side of Connor excited her.

"Nay, leave it off. I like looking," she admitted with a giggle.

That got a smile out of him, and it did her heart good to see it.

"When you invited me here today, I didn't think I'd be doing this," admitted Connor.

"Oh. Did you want to stop? It wasn't my intention to make you do manual labor."

"Nay, I don't mind," he said. "It feels good and takes my mind off my troubles."

"Speaking of that, how is your father?" She walked over to the far side of the garden, closer to the barn.

"Stubborn as all hell. But if you mean his health, it's no better."

"I can't understand why Rose isn't here by now. Something must have happened."

"It's fine," he said, continuing to dig.

"What's wrong, Connor? I can see it on your face. Something is really troubling you."

"It's nothing."

"Please. You can tell me."

"Oh, all right. I had a heated conversation with my father this morning and I'm still bothered by it."

"Really? What happened?"

"My father wants to start taking Leoric to executions," he said, digging even faster.

It seemed to Eleanor that the more he worried, the faster he worked.

"And that bothers you?" she asked, already knowing the answer, but wanting him to tell her.

"Yes, of course it bothers me. My brother can't handle cleaning out garderobes without throwing up. What do you think will happen the first time he has to assist with an execution? It's not easy you know."

"Nay. I don't suppose it is. After all, it is hard enough just to watch as a spectator." She walked closer and sat on a log near him to continue talking while he dug up the earth.

"Connor, there must be a way to get you and your siblings out of this mess you're in."

"I don't see how," he told her. "My father sealed our fate the day he bartered for his life."

"You need to forgive him for that. Any man would have done the same thing in his position. Especially when he had five children to support and had just lost his wife."

Connor finished digging, throwing the shovel to the side, and wiping the sweat off his brow with the back of his arm. "He's not the one I can't forgive."

When Eleanor realized he was talking about himself, she knew she needed to get him to a private place.

"I think Edna keeps a water barrel and ladle in the barn. Why don't we take a walk and get you a drink? You must be thirsty."

"Yes, I could go for some water."

He picked up his tunic, but didn't put it on. Together, they walked to the barn. Eleanor was glad everyone else was out picking peas, because she really wanted time alone with Connor, and it was so hard to come by.

Once they were inside the barn, Connor draped his tunic over the post of a stall and scooped out a ladle of water, holding it out to her. "Do you want some?"

"No, thank you. I'm fine."

He proceeded to drink, helping himself to several ladles of water, pouring the last one in his hand and splashing it on his face. The water ran in rivulets down his bare chest. Eleanor's eyes eagerly followed.

"You blame yourself for what happened," she said, still staring at his chest.

"I do," he admitted. "I was young and didn't know what decision to make. But the one I made wasn't fair to you."

He put back the ladle and reached out and gently stroked the side of her face.

"Nay, it wasn't," she whispered, a hitch in her breath. Her eyes interlocked with his. "But you did the only thing you could. It wouldn't have been right to reject the offer. Then you and your siblings would have had to watch your father be beheaded."

"I suppose so. But if I had made the opposite choice, we'd all still be nobles right now."

"And your father would be dead."

"I'd be a knight and married to you, Eleanor. But I'm not. That is my biggest regret."

Before she knew what happened, he had pulled her up against his hot, wet chest and wrapped his strong arms around her. Then his mouth came down against hers and he kissed her hard, the kiss filled with passion.

She let him kiss her, liking the way it felt. And when her curiosity got the best of her, she reached out and touched his bare skin, running her hands down his chest ever so slowly.

He broke the kiss with a gasp. At first she thought she'd somehow hurt him.

"I'm sorry," she said, pulling her hands away.

"Nay, don't stop. I like being touched by you, Eleanor." He put her hands back on his chest and kissed her once again.

Feeling each taut muscle under her fingertips, she slid her hands lower and lower.

A moan lodged at the back of his throat when her fingers landed at the top of his breeches. It excited her to hear his vocal pleasure. It made her feel lusty. Then, when he kissed her again, one of his hands slid down her neck, his fingertips skimming the bare skin of her collarbone. Then his hand slid down to her upper chest. Her heart beat faster as he got closer to her breasts. To her delight, he cupped one of her breasts and squeezed gently, using his thumb to rub her nipple right through her gown.

"Oh!" she gasped, breathing deeper and harder.

"Did you like that?" he asked, whispering into her ear, nibbling at her lobe as he spoke. It was followed by a quick lick of his tongue.

Her eyes closed and her knees became weak from want. She collapsed against him, feeling so hot right now that she couldn't even speak. So instead she nodded.

"You are so beautiful and such a full-fledged woman." His hands cupped her buttocks now. "You have no idea how many nights I wake up hard, wanting nothing more than to slide my manhood between your hot thighs, burying myself to the hilt until you scream out my name."

Hearing this made Eleanor squirm in his embrace. His words were causing her to come alive in a very sexual manner.

He kissed her passionately again, this time pulling her hips against his. When he did, she could feel his engorged manhood bulging out from under his trews. It intrigued her, but scared her at the same time.

"Connor," she said, hearing how seductive and breathy she sounded, even if she hadn't meant to do it. As much as she liked this, she was getting too aroused. So, she pushed away from him and fixed her gown. Her eyes darted out the door of the barn. Thankfully, everyone was still out in the field.

She heard him curse softly under his breath. "I'm so sorry, Eleanor. Please forgive me. I got carried away. I didn't mean to do that."

"We both got carried away," she said. "But I want you to know, I am not pushing you away to stop you."

"You're not?" he asked, seeming really confused.

Her breathing deepened and her heart pounded harder. Her gaze shot up to the hayloft over their heads. "I think we should continue this, but not here. Let's find somewhere no one will see us. The hayloft might be a good place."

He stared at her again with those hooded eyes that were undressing her though he wasn't even touching her. Her anticipation became unbearable, and she didn't know how much more of this she could take before she shattered. But she needed to touch him. She wanted him to touch her. God's eyes, she prayed he would not reject her offer.

"Is that what you want, Eleanor? What you really want?" he asked, seeming like he wanted her to be sure.

She nodded silently, her tongue flicking out to lick her dry lips. His gaze settled on her mouth and he moaned deeply once again. "You are driving me mad."

"Isn't it what you want too?" she asked him.

"More than you'll ever know."

"Then I suggest we hurry. The others will be back soon."

Without another word, they hurried up the ladder to the hayloft. Kissing passionately, he wasted no time in undressing her, while she did the same to him. It was happening. She was finally going to make love with Connor. This is what she'd been dreaming about for years now.

"You won't regret this, Eleanor, will you?" he asked, as if either of them could really stop right now. She was so hot and eager to make love with him that she boldly pushed him down in the hay.

"Just try and stop right now and see what I do. That should give you your answer."

He chuckled and pulled her down atop him, kissing her, slipping his tongue into her mouth.

She loved the feeling of having part of Connor inside her. It felt alluring, and right. It only made her more anxious to make love with this man—the only man she'd ever loved.

"I promise, I'll be gentle," he told her, cupping her cheek and brushing his thumb over her lips. "Although, it's been a while since I found my release, and I can't promise how long I can make this last. Has it been a long time for you, too?"

"I've never made love with a man before, Connor."

"Nay?" He raised a brow.

"This will be my first time."

"My dear, sweet Eleanor. You didn't have to wait for me. What if this never happened?"

"Then I suppose I'd end up being a nun after all," she said with a smile.

"Mmmm," he mumbled, pulling her off of him and taking the place of aggressor. "I don't want to hear anything else about being a nun. It's going to kill the mood."

She giggled. "I promise," she whispered, feeling his hand trail down her neck to her chest. Their eyes remained locked.

"You are so beautiful, my dear." He wrapped his fingers around one breast and then lowered his mouth and pleasured her with his tongue against her nipple. Her nipple hardened to a small bud and Connor took her into his mouth.

"Oh!" she cried out, feeling a tingling sensation go through her. As he continued to suckle her, she found her back arching upward, pushing her breast further into his hot mouth. She grabbed on to his long, dark hair, squeezing her eyes closed tightly, not wanting to let him go.

"Connor, this feels so good."

"This is only the foreplay," he told her, skimming his hand over her body while he held himself up with the other. "The first thing we need to do is to prepare you. It will feel even better if you are ready."

He used his hand to cup her womanhood, slipping a finger in between her folds.

"Ooooh," she moaned as he entered her.

"Mmmm," he said, flicking his finger in and out, each time going a little deeper.

Eleanor squirmed in ecstasy beneath him, basking in the delightful feeling coursing through her body from the way he used his hand to bring her to life. Her body vibrated and she felt the start of some movement deep in her core. She wanted more of him. She wanted all of him and could wait no longer. "I am ready, Connor," she said, breathing harder and harder. Her body felt like it was on fire. His bare skin pressed up against her made her feel as if they were melding into one. She loved every minute of it. "Make love to me, now. Please," she begged, feeling the slight trembling of her body. She did not tremble because she was frightened. It was the excitement coursing through her that took control.

"Not yet," he said, this time mounting her, spreading his legs around her hips. Her eyes fastened on the beautiful package dangling above her. He used both arms to hold up his body as he slowly lowered himself to her. Rubbing his engorged manhood against her, she was able to feel his manly power. Her gaze swept downward once again and she moaned in pleasure. Curiosity got the best of her and she reached between them, touching him, needing to know how he would feel in her hand. Wrapping her fingers around his hardened form, she gave his form a slight squeeze, reveling in the excitement of feeling soft silk over hardened steel.

"Easy, sweetheart," he told her in a deep voice. "I've been dreaming of making love to you for so long that I don't want to get there before you."

"Before me?" she asked. "But we're together."

"I want us both to feel the joy of finding our release at the same time." He reached down to fondle her again and gave a slight nod. "Aye, I think you're ready now."

Then ever so slowly, he slipped his hardened form into her, making sure she wasn't uncomfortable before he continued. She watched as they joined together, finally becoming one.

When he'd entered her completely, a smile spread across her face. She was no longer frightened about making love because she felt as if they fit together perfectly and this is how it was meant to be.

Connor's hips started to move and so did hers as they met each other over and over again.

They did the dance of love as he thrust into her and pulled back out, each time making her more and more excited. It didn't take long for her to learn how to move to please him like he was pleasing her. And then a feeling overcame her that she'd never felt before.

"Oh, Connor, something is happening."

"Let loose, Eleanor. Don't hold back."

They both found their release, their hot bodies pressed deliciously together as they rose to the highest heights, finding the passion that she always knew was there. They held each other tightly in a lovers' embrace. Then the feeling subsided and they parted, but lay next to each other in the hay, holding each other, kissing, and making Eleanor wish this would never end.

"That was... better than I'd ever imagined," he told her.

"It was wonderful, Connor. We belong together. Always."

Before he could answer, she heard a lot of commotion and got up and looked out the window of the hayloft to see Albert driving the wagon back from the field with his wife, Lark and Raven, the children, and the dog as well. With them was someone that Eleanor had not expected to see.

"Rose. It's Rose! And Rook," said Eleanor. "They're here. Now we can heal your father. Hurry, we need to get dressed."

They both dressed quickly and headed down the ladder. He was first and helped her so she wouldn't slip on the rungs.

"Fast, don your tunic," she told him, picking it up and tossing it to him. Their eyes interlocked again, and she gave him one more kiss for now, hoping it wouldn't be the last time she ever kissed him.

She ran out to greet Rose and Rook, just as lightning slashed across the sky and thunder boomed overhead.

"Let's get this wagon into the barn before the peas get wet and moldy," called out Albert, driving.

The sky opened up and rain pelted down just as the wagon entered the barn.

"Children, get into the house, and take Roger," called out Edna, trying to herd them to the cottage door. "Everyone, follow me."

"The house is small. The rest of us can wait in the barn until the rain let's up," suggested Eleanor. "Rose and Rook, I am so glad you are finally here."

Lark, Raven, Rook, and Rose stayed in the barn. Albert was there, as well as Connor.

Eleanor gave Rose a hug. "I'm so glad you came."

"I spotted them on the road and called them over," announced Lark.

"I would have come sooner, but Rook insisted I wait for him to finish up some business."

"That's right," said Rook. "I was not about to let my wife go anywhere without me at her side."

"Where is the castle guard?" asked Raven curiously.

"I sent him back to Blake Castle since he was no longer needed," said Rook, noticing Connor standing there. "You're the hangman," he said.

"Rook, this is Connor Wyland," Eleanor told him. "You remember him, don't you? I was betrothed to him as a child."

"Oh, I know exactly who he is," said Rook, looking him up and down.

"Eleanor, I was told to come immediately and that someone needed my help," said Rose. "What is this all about?"

"Connor's father is sick. Because he is the hangman, no one will administer help to him in any way," explained Eleanor. "You know a lot about herbs, Rose, so I was hoping you could help him."

"You want my wife to help the hangman?" Rook didn't sound at all happy about this idea.

"Well, I was hoping there was something she could do." Eleanor wasn't feeling so hopeful anymore.

"Of course, I can," said Rose, but Rook did not agree.

"Rose, you are doing no such thing. I don't want you near the hangman and his family."

"Rook, stop it," Raven told her twin brother. "Connor is a good man and he needs our help."

"We are nobles. We won't be helping a hangman or his family," were Rook's final words.

"I didn't think you would, Lord Rook. After all, you don't usually even talk to anyone from below the salt." Connor glared back at him.

"That's not true," protested Rose. "Rook married me, and I was just a commoner."

"Connor just pulled a heavy plow off my leg and dug up my

entire garden," Albert told them, struggling to get out of the wagon. "I agree with Eleanor. He is a good man."

Connor hurried over to him. "I'll help you to the house, Albert," he said, putting his arm around the injured man.

"I have to kill a chicken for our meal first. Mayhap two since we have so many guests," said Albert.

"I'll do it for you," offered Connor, causing everyone to become quiet. "After all, isn't that what executioners do?" he asked snidely, staring at Rook.

"There's no need. We're not staying," said Rook.

"Why not?" asked Rose. "I would like to accept their kind invitation."

"So would I," said Raven. "We've worked up an appetite harvesting the peas."

"God's eyes, Raven. We are nobles," Rook scolded her. "You need to stop doing the jobs of peasants. You shouldn't be out in the fields at all. You should be sewing in the ladies' solar instead."

"Brother, I am usually out in the practice yard with my weapons, so don't think I'm going to listen to you when you tell me not to do something. Besides, I thought you changed when you married Rose. I didn't think you'd still be acting so high and mighty."

"Excuse me, Lord Noble," said Connor, helping Albert to walk, exiting the barn. He stopped and called back over his shoulder. "Don't worry about helping my father. After all, nobles shouldn't be seen with commoners. Especially not with such a low-life like me."

He walked to the house with Albert. Eleanor felt the tears welling up in her eyes. As soon as he left, she walked over and slapped Rook across the face.

"What the hell was that all about?" asked Rook, holding his stinging cheek.

"That's for the way you treated Connor when he didn't deserve it."

Raven walked over and slapped her brother next.

"Raven, this isn't funny," growled Rook, his anger growing.

"That is for being a pompous ass," said Raven, walking away.

"My turn," said Lark, reaching out and slapping him across the face as well.

"And what was that for, dear Cousin?" asked Rook, scowling.

"No reason. I just wanted to get in on the fun," giggled Lark, making Rose giggle as well.

"I'll help Connor's father, don't worry," Rose told her. "But first, I'd like to accept their invitation and stay for dinner. It seems to mean a lot to them, and I don't want to disappoint them by leaving now."

"I agree. I want to stay to eat, too," said Raven.

"A meal for all of us? In that little cottage?" Rook looked out the door into the pouring rain. "We won't all fit inside."

"Then we'll make up a table out here in the barn," suggested Eleanor.

"We're going to eat with the animals?" asked Rook, blowing air from his mouth. "I don't think so."

"I knew I should have left you back at Rookrose Manor, husband," said Rose. "Now, stop giving us trouble. Eleanor, I will help you set up a table right here in the barn."

"Word of this better never get out. Do you all understand?" asked Rook.

"That's better. Thank you, dear," said Rose, giving him a quick kiss on the cheek.

Eleanor's heart swelled. This was so wrong for nobles to eat with peasants, especially out in a barn of all places. It was even worse that they were going to eat with an executioner, but she didn't care.

Everything about this was preposterous.

The only thing she couldn't understand was that if it was so wrong, then why in the world did it feel so right?

CHAPTER 12

By the time it had stopped raining and they had finished eating, it was nearly nightfall.

"Eleanor, as much as I enjoyed this, I really need to get home to my family," said Connor.

"Yes, I agree. Rose, are you ready to go?" asked Eleanor.

"I am," said Rose, saying her goodbyes to the family.

"I'm tired," said little Lena with a big yawn.

"Can't our sisters live here with us too?" asked Hamlin.

"They're not our sisters, you idiot," said Bertram.

"But you're our brothers," Margaret told them. "And I like it here better than at the abbey."

"Can we stay with you, Mrs. Woods?" Lena clung to the woman's leg.

"Oh, I wish you girls could stay with us," said Edna.

"I can barely feed the two boys now," grumbled Albert, sitting at the table in the cottage with his hurt foot wrapped and propped up on a chair. "The boys are really too young to be of much help. I'm afraid Lord Sampson will run us out of here if he finds out that I'm hurt and can't work for a while. We will never be able to keep up with the chores."

"What are we going to do?" asked Edna, wiping away a tear.

"I'll return to help you until you're back on your feet," said Connor, not liking to see Edna and Albert in trouble.

"You can't be doing our work for us. It's not right," said Albert.

"I have a brother that I'll bring with me. Between the two of us, we'll get a lot of work done."

"But aren't you forgetting you have another job?" asked Rook.

Connor's head snapped around. "There are no executions planned for any time soon, if that is what you're asking."

"We appreciate your offer, but we can't pay you," said Edna. "All we can do is give you food for your family."

"Fair enough," said Connor with a nod. "Thank you, but I must be on my way now." He pulled his cloak on and covered his head with the hood.

"Eleanor, we really should get the girls back to the abbey before dark," said Lark.

"I agree," said Raven. "Lark and I will take them back in the wagon. Eleanor, you need to go with the others to help Connor's father."

"I won't let women and girls travel alone. I'm coming with you," said Rook. "Afterwards, I will escort Rose and Eleanor to the hangman's house."

"Nay, it'll be dark by then," said Eleanor. "And we've already waited too long. His father needs our help now. You go back to the abbey with the others. Connor will be with us to protect us."

Rook didn't like that idea, but Rose told him he was being too overprotective and sent him and the others on their way.

"I brought my horse. You'll have to ride with me," Eleanor told Connor.

"I'm not sure that's a good idea, sweetheart."

She mounted the horse and nodded to him. "Come on, Connor. We're in a hurry. This is no time to be shy. Let's get to your father and help him. We can't wait for you to walk while we ride."

"That's right," agreed Rose. "This will be faster."

"I'VE NEVER BEEN CALLED shy, and I never will be again." Connor pulled himself up into the saddle behind Eleanor, wrapping his arms around her. They rode back to his cottage with their bodies pressed together. It was only making him feel aroused, and he wondered if he'd made a mistake by picking up the gauntlet when Eleanor so boldly threw it down at his feet, accusing him of being shy. Perhaps this was her intention all along.

"I enjoyed our time together today," he said softly, up against her ear. When Rose wasn't looking, he sneaked her a quick kiss on the back of her neck.

"Oh, Connor, you have no idea how much this day meant to me." Eleanor giggled when he kissed her neck. She smelled like rosewater, something he hadn't smelled since the day he left the castle. Her hair was vibrant like flames of fire, but soft as silk, too. A few strands blew in the wind and brushed up against his face and he loved it.

"Dammit, you are driving me crazy, woman."

"And you, me," came her answer.

As much as he was enjoying this ride with Eleanor, he had a feeling deep in his gut that his happiness wouldn't last. That feeling was validated when they rode up to his cottage. He heard crying coming from inside the house. Outside, their wagon was filled with hay... and blood.

"Oh, hell, no." Connor slid off the horse and held up his arms to help her dismount. He helped Rose as well.

"Connor, what's the matter?" asked Eleanor.

"The wagon." He nodded toward it.

"Is that—blood?" asked Rose.

"It's been used for an execution and it hasn't been cleaned yet. Dammit, what is going on here?"

Connor stormed to the door of the cottage and threw it open to find Ginevra sitting by the fire with her arm around Alaric and they were both crying. Leoric was sitting in a dark corner with his arms around himself, muttering nonsense, rocking back and forth. Connor didn't see his father anywhere.

"What the hell is going on here?" Connor quickly lit a lantern. When the firelight lit up the room, he realized Leoric's body was shaking. There was a puddle of vomit at his feet.

"Leoric? What the hell happened to you?"

"I tried to help him since you weren't here. It was awful, Connor. There was so much blood." Leoric's eyes closed and he shivered once again.

"Where's Father?" asked Connor.

Leoric looked to the bedroom door and nodded.

"I'll take Rose to him. Mayhap we can help." Eleanor hurried to the bedroom with Rose.

"There was no execution planned today," spat Connor. "So what are you talking about? Where did you two go?"

"Lord Sampson's guard came to the door early this morning and said we needed to go to the castle for an execution." Leoric continued to shake. "I told Father I would help him since he was ill and you weren't here. It was a... a beheading, Connor." His brother actually started to cry.

"God's eyes, I never should have left. Ginevra, Alaric, why are you two crying?"

"He's dead," sobbed Ginevra.

"What? Who's dead?" asked Connor, thinking at first she was talking about the executed man.

"Father is dead," wailed little Alaric.

"Bid the devil, tell me this isn't so." Connor ran to the bedroom and burst inside. Rose and Eleanor were standing over the bed with a lit candle, looking down at the bed. His father lay there, not moving. His eyes were wide open, staring into nothingness, as if in fear. "Is he—is he dead?" Connor walked closer to the bed.

"I'm sorry," said Rose, reaching out and closing his father's eyes. "I should have come sooner. It's my fault."

"Nay, Rose," said Eleanor. "It's no one's fault. There was probably nothing you could have done anyway."

"Nay. This can't be happening." Connor stormed from the room and headed over to Leoric. "What happened to Father?"

"I-I don't know," said the boy.

"Tell me!" Connor pulled him up by the front of his tunic and slapped him across the face. "Snap out of this and talk to me, dammit. Tell me everything that happened."

Leoric, blinked a few times and shook his head. Then he slowly dropped his arms to his sides. "It was a beheading," he said softly.

"I know that part, dammit. How did Father die?"

"He was weak and he wanted me to do it."

"God's eyes, nay. Please tell me you didn't."

"I-I wanted to help him. I wanted to be strong like him. Like you. I told him I could take your place, Connor, but I couldn't do it."

"Did Father carry out the execution?"

"Yes. But since he was so weak it-it took him several tries to complete it."

Connor closed his eyes and let out a deep breath. This must have been awful. Especially for Leoric who had never assisted in an execution before.

"What did Lord Sampson do?" Executioners botching beheadings wasn't something that was easily accepted. Sometimes they were even killed for not doing the job right the first time.

"He wasn't happy at first. But then he called Father to him and he gave him a chalice to drink from."

"He did what?" Connor started to pace. "That makes no sense at all. Why would he do that?"

"I-I don't know. I had to leave to bury the body. Lord Sampson made me bury the chalice as well. When I returned, Father said he felt ill and wanted to get home right away. I drove as fast as I could. But-but he died in the wagon, Connor." Leoric's eyes filled with tears. "He was gasping for breath and I didn't know how to help him. So I put him in bed when we got here but-but he never woke up."

Eleanor and Rose hurried over to comfort the younger children.

"I'll dig a grave for him outside the cottage," said Connor heading for the door. "I'll put him next to Francesca."

It took every bit of Connor's strength not to cry as well. If he hadn't been so angry about what happened, he just might have broken down. Instead, he went to the shed and got a shovel and started digging a grave next to his sister in the woods.

"Connor," said Eleanor, coming to his side. "I'm so sorry."

"What for?" he asked, digging the hole like a madman.

"If I hadn't asked you to meet me and you hadn't stayed so

long at the Woods' house, mayhap none of this would have happened."

"I blame no one but that wretched bastard, Sampson. He is supposed to give us at least two days' notice for executions. It's like he wanted this to happen, I swear."

"As soon as Rook returns, I think we should take your siblings to the abbey for the night. It's not healthy for them to stay here right now."

"Well, they're orphans now, and your job is to take in orphans, so how can I stop you?"

"Rose and Rook will be staying there as well, in the guest house. I'd like you to come to the abbey for the night as well."

"Nay!" He shouted. "I won't leave my father. I should have been here to help him and I wasn't. I was off pretending to be something and someone I wasn't. If I had been here my father would still be alive and my brother wouldn't be going crazy from what he saw today. This never should have happened."

"Please, Connor. It's not anyone's fault."

"Eleanor?" called out Rose, coming to join them. "The children are crying and scared of me since they don't know me. Will you help me convince them to pack a few things and to come to the abbey with us?"

"Yes," said Eleanor, looking at Connor and sighing deeply. "But I don't want to leave before Connor's father is buried."

ROOK RETURNED to the cottage with Raven, since Raven knew the way to get there. It was already dark and lanterns burned outside. Conner had taken care of the horse and finished cleaning out the wagon and digging his father's grave.

"What's going on here?" asked Raven, getting off her horse.

"Come here," said Eleanor. "Come inside and I'll tell you everything."

They buried Wensel Wyland in the dark, with Connor and Leoric filling in the grave. Rook had offered to do it, but Connor and his brother wanted to do this one last thing for their father.

"I'd like us all to hold hands and say a prayer for Wensel's soul," said Eleanor after the burying was completed. No one objected. They held hands in a circle around the grave, praying out loud.

When Connor saw Alaric yawn, he walked over and picked up his little brother. "Alaric, you and Ginevra and Leoric are going to spend the night at the abbey."

"Are you coming with us?" asked Alaric.

"Nay. I am going to stay here. I need some time alone."

"I want to stay here with you," said Leoric.

"Me too," said Ginevra clinging to Connor.

"Leoric, I'm counting on you to watch over our younger brother and sister," said Connor. "It will do you good to get away from here for the night."

"Nay. We can all stay here together, Connor," protested Leoric.

"I'm in charge now that Father is gone," said Connor. "Now please, go with them. Be there for Ginevra and Alaric. I will meet up with all of you tomorrow."

"All right," said Leoric. "Come on, Ginevra and Alaric. I'll watch over you. You don't need to be afraid."

"Now that Father is gone, does Connor have to be the one to murder people?" asked Alaric, almost breaking Connor's heart. Is this really the way his little brother thought of him? Is it how he thought of their father? That he was nothing but a murderer?

No one said a word.

"I'm not going to be a murderer, and neither was Father," said Connor in a steady voice.

"Please, don't die and leave us too," said Ginevra, once again clinging to him and crying.

"Stop it," he told his sister, trying to be strong. "I'm not going to die. I'm going to see all of you tomorrow. But right now, you need to go to the abbey with Lady Eleanor and the others and get a good night's sleep."

"I'm hungry," said Alaric with another yawn.

"Lady Eleanor will make sure you get something to eat as well," said Connor. "Now go!"

"Connor," said Eleanor, pulling him to the side. "I want to stay here with you tonight."

"Absolutely not!"

"You shouldn't be alone at a time like this. It's much better if someone is here with you. You'll need someone to talk to."

"I'm done talking," he told her. "I know you mean well, Eleanor, but please just take my siblings and leave. All I want is to be alone right now."

"As you wish," she said, gathering up the children. "Should we take the wagon?"

"Nay," he said, not wanting his siblings riding in it right now, even though he'd cleaned it out. It symbolized death and filth, and he didn't want them near it.

"There are three of us and three of them," said Raven. "We can each ride double. It'll be fine."

Finally, they all left. Connor looked down to his father's grave once more, shaking his head. "How could you let this happen? Why the hell did you take Leoric with you? Don't you see what you did to him? He wasn't strong enough to handle this. You scarred the poor boy for life."

He stormed into the house, angry at Lord Sampson, angry at his father, and angry at himself. He kicked over a bench and then with a swipe of his hand, threw all the plates and cups from the table to the ground. He went over and used the poker to stoke the fire. Staring at it in his hand, the burn on his face started to ache. He looked at the hot poker in his hand and he felt like he was sixteen all over again. Cries and shouts echoed in his head. He saw his father about to be beheaded, kneeling down with his hands tied behind his back, waiting for Connor to decide his fate. Then he felt the hot iron from the forge burning into his face and he even smelled the scent of his own burning skin.

"Nay! Dammit!" He threw down the poker and headed to the bedroom, needing to clear his crowded mind. He pushed open the door almost expecting to see his drunken father lying on the bed, but he wasn't there. Connor went over to his father's trunk and dug inside, his hand closing around the neck of a bottle of whisky.

Sitting on the floor, he uncorked the bottle and raised the it to his mouth, guzzling down the golden liquid. It felt like his lungs were on fire and as if he had just entered hell.

He lowered the bottle and laughed. Now he knew exactly how his father had felt. With his father dead, Connor was the town's new hangman. He looked down and fingered the dagger at his side, thinking it was too hard for him to execute another man, but felt it would be so easy to kill himself right now.

He slugged down more whisky, drinking until he couldn't see straight. Then he removed his waist belt with his weapon and pouch and threw it on the floor. He plucked the dagger from his waist belt and held the tip of the blade to his chest.

"I don't want this life and neither do I need it," he said, knowing there was only one way to escape this life of hell once and for all. Sadly, once again, he was the one who had to make that awful decision.

CHAPTER 13

Eleanor approached Connor's home the following morning, having been escorted by her cousin Raven with her sword. They left the abbey early, before the rest of their cousins awoke. Eleanor hadn't slept a wink all night, thinking about Connor and what he must be going through right now. She only wanted to comfort him. To be a friend. To give him someone to talk to. To be his strength right now.

"Thank you for escorting me, Raven. I know Rook would tell me to stay away from Connor right now, but this is exactly when he needs me the most."

"He's in a bad situation," said Raven as they rode. The sun poked its head up over the horizon. "I mean, now that his father is dead, he is the hangman, you realize."

"He doesn't want to execute people." Eleanor felt emotions welling within her. "All he wants to is be a knight and noble. The way he should be."

"That's nothing we can change about his situation, Eleanor, so don't even try. Connor made the decision to save his father's life and in doing so, it sealed the fate for his entire family. Now he needs to learn to live with it."

"It's just not fair," said Eleanor, shaking her head, unable to believe the wicked turn of events. "Yesterday we were all having fun at the home of Edna and Albert. It almost seemed like the old times when we grew up with Connor."

"Don't let that fool you. Nothing has changed. Just remember this when you go in to talk to him."

"He needs to be comforted."

They stopped their horses in front of Connor's cottage.

"Comforted, yes. But please don't bed him. It wouldn't be a good choice for either of you right now."

"I have no intention of taking advantage of his vulnerable state. Now, stay here while I go in alone. I think it will be too overwhelming if both of us go in to see him."

"I'll be waiting," said Raven, scanning the area like any good warrior would do. "Just don't be too long. I want to get back before Rook awakes. My brother won't be as under-standing as I am about all this."

"I know, I know. I'll hurry."

Eleanor dismounted and went up to Connor's door, knocking softly. When he didn't answer, she knocked a little louder.

"Connor?" she called out. "It's me. Eleanor. Connor are you in there?"

She looked back at Raven and shrugged.

"See if the door is unlocked," Raven told her.

Eleanor tried the door and it opened. "Connor?" She stuck her head into the darkened room, looking around. "Good morning," she called out, taking a step inside.

She suddenly got the awful feeling something was wrong. Walking into the cottage, she stopped when something crunched under her feet. That's when she realized the table and benches were turned over and things were scattered everywhere. It looked like possibly there had been a struggle.

She was about to go back outside and get Raven when she thought she heard Connor's voice from the bedroom. She tiptoed over and slowly pushed open the door. The bed was empty. No one was there.

"Connor?" she said again. She was about to turn around and leave when she saw what looked like a person lying on the floor on the opposite side of the bed, and it looked like Connor. "Is that you?" she asked, heading over. When she gazed down to the floor she saw Connor with his eyes closed, holding an empty bottle of whisky. In his other hand he gripped his dagger and also her green hair ribbon. The blade of the dagger was covered with dried blood.

"Nay! Connor!" She threw her body over him and started wailing. "What did you do? Why did you kill yourself?" She hugged his prone body.

"What the hell is going on?" came his deep grumble.

She sat back up and pushed the hair from her eyes. "Connor! You're not dead! Thank goodness!" She reached over and started kissing him on the mouth. He smelled and tasted strongly from whisky.

"God's eyes, Eleanor, what are you doing here?" He sat up, trying to get his bearings.

"I came to comfort you and you didn't answer the knock at your door. I thought you were dead when I saw that bloody dagger in your hand."

"Huh?" He looked down and shook his head, putting down the blade as well as the bottle, but holding up the green ribbon in front of his face. "I can't lie. I thought about killing myself last night when I was in a drunken stupor. But then I saw your green hair ribbon fall out of my pouch and I knew I couldn't leave you."

"Oh, is that the one I dropped at the hanging?"

"Yes," he told her, lowering it to his lap.

"Well, why is there blood on your dagger?"

"I killed a rat last night that was bothering me." He nodded and she saw the dead rat under the bed and screamed.

"Shhhh," he said, making a face and holding his hands up to his ears. "You are too loud for the middle of the night."

"Middle of the night?" she asked. "Nay, Connor, it's morning. Look." She ran over and pulled open the shutter, letting the first rays of sunlight stream into the room.

"Ooooh, too bright," he moaned, getting to his feet, still clutching her hair ribbon.

"Eleanor, I heard you scream. Is everything all right?" asked Raven from outside. She was off her horse and next to the window with her sword already unsheathed.

"Yes, everything is fine, Raven. It was just a dead rat that frightened me," she told her cousin.

"Oh. All right." Raven sheathed her sword and walked back to her horse.

"Why did you come here?" he asked, staggering to the kitchen. Eleanor followed right behind him. "You should be with my siblings at the abbey."

"They are fine," she told him. "But I wasn't so sure about you."

"Well, as you can see, I'm still here." He held up his palms and when he did, the ribbon he was holding fell to the floor.

"I know. But I was so scared," she said picking up the ribbon. "I thought you'd possibly been attached when I saw everything so disheveled." She motioned to the overturned table and benches.

"And yet you still ventured into the house by yourself? Was that a smart thing to do?"

"I-I suppose not. But all I could think about was you. You were so upset when we left here last night."

"Do you blame me? It was one hell of a day."

"Nay, not at all. I just didn't want you to be alone."

"Oh." He ran a hand through his long hair and righted the table and then picked up the benches and sat down. "Now I'm the damned hangman, since my father is gone."

"Nay, Conner." She sat down next to him and covered his hand with her own. "Please don't even say that."

"Well, it's true. Just the thought of it would make anyone want to kill themselves."

"I'm glad you stopped and didn't go through with it. I'm happy you decided not to leave this world after all."

"Eleanor, I don't care about my life anymore. That's not what kept me from taking my life, I told you. It was because of you. Also, because I kept thinking of my brother Leoric, and how terrified he was after assisting with the beheading yesterday."

"Yes, he did seem very upset."

"If I were to kill myself, that would mean Leoric would have to take the position of hangman. He could never handle it. I couldn't lay that burden on his shoulders the way my father laid it on mine."

"Connor, what are you going to do? I know you're the executioner now, but I don't want to believe it," she said softly.

"Neither do I." He patted his chest, pulling out a metal flask from under his tunic. He uncorked the flask and raised it to his lips. Only a few drops of whisky came out. "Dammit," he shouted, throwing the container across the room.

"Drinking more won't solve your problems."

"Nay, but I see now why my father spent all our money on whisky. It was the only way he could get through all the voices in his head taunting him because of what he had to do."

"What's going to happen now?" she asked. "I know you don't want to kill anyone."

"I have no choice. As soon as the soldiers show up at my door with the order of an execution, I'll have to carry it out."

"Couldn't you refuse to do it?" she asked.

"Hah!" He got up and started pacing the room. "Not if I don't want them coming after my siblings to try to get me to do the job."

"None of this is right," she cried, getting up and walking over to him. "Connor, I don't want you to be the hangman." She took his hands in hers.

Just then, the door opened and Raven stuck her head inside the cottage.

"Excuse me for interrupting, but there is someone here for Connor."

"Not now," said Connor, angry that anyone was bothering him at a time like this. It was all he could do just to talk with Eleanor. He didn't want to see anyone else. "Tell them I'm not up for seeing visitors."

"Uh, I don't think I can do that," said Raven, seeming very uncomfortable.

"Why not?" asked Eleanor.

"Because we're not here for a friendly visit." A man pushed Raven aside and threw the door open wide.

Connor's jaw dropped when he saw two of Lord Sampson's guards standing there. A third one was behind them, struggling with someone, but he couldn't see who it was.

"What the hell do you want?" asked Connor.

"We're here to see the hangman," said the second guard. "Where is your father?"

Connor's gaze flashed over to Eleanor who looked as terrified as he felt at the moment. He didn't want her to say anything, so he spoke.

"He's not here," said Connor.

"When will he be back?" asked the guard.

"Why do you want to know?" Connor felt a knot forming in the pit of his stomach.

"We caught a thief and Lord Sampson wants all thieves executed at once," said the man.

"Well, he's not here. He can't do it," snapped Connor.

"It is his job. He has to comply. Now where is he?"

"Dammit, my father won't be executing anyone, because he's dead!"

"Oh," said the first guard with a shrug. "Well, then I guess you'll just have to do it. Be at the castle first thing in the morning for the hanging."

"Wait," said Eleanor as they started to leave. "Tell me, who is this thief that you are so fast to execute?"

"He's no one important. Just a damned filthy peasant boy."

"Boy?" asked Eleanor.

"Aye," said the guards, moving aside so she could see the third guard with the prisoner. "He's right there."

When they stepped apart, Connor looked past them and his heart sank. The third guard held a teenaged boy by the tunic. The boy's arms were tied behind him. It was hard enough having to assume the position of hangman, but now, the first person he would be required to execute was someone he already knew.

Eleanor gasped and held her hand to her mouth.

"Please, don't kill me," cried the boy.

Connor stepped out the door and bit his bottom lip, shaking his head. "Dammit, Finnian, why the hell couldn't you stop stealing? Now, I'm going to have to kill you."

CHAPTER 14

"Nay! Let the boy go," shouted Eleanor, pushing past Connor and running out to hug Finnian.

"Get away from him. He's a murdering thief," spat the guard, pushing her away and keeping her from touching the boy.

"Murdering thief?" Her heart beat furiously and her head snapped around. "Finnian, did you kill someone?"

"Nay, I swear, I didn't," cried the boy.

"Well, he stabbed one of our guards in the leg right after he was caught stealing his money pouch," said the guard holding Finnian. He nodded to a fourth castle guard sitting atop his horse with a bloody cloth wrapped around his leg.

"I only did it because the guard started choking me," protested Finnian with wide eyes. "Lady Eleanor, please help me. I promise I'll never steal anything from anyone ever again."

"Too late for that," sneered the guard. "Now we'll have a hanging for the Autumn Festival. That should please Lord Sampson greatly. The crowds like it when a prisoner is executed. It will be entertaining for them."

"Entertaining? You are a monster!" yelled Eleanor. "I won't let you kill him. He's just a boy. He didn't mean to hurt anyone and you heard him say he'll never steal again."

"Do you really expect us to believe that?" asked the first guard, who had come to the door. "We've been after this thief for quite some time now. Thank goodness we finally caught him."

"Aye," said the guard with him. "It's just one more filthy, no-good, ragpicker out of our way."

"Please, Connor. Don't kill the boy," begged Eleanor. "I'll watch over him. I'll take him back to the abbey with me and make sure he never causes trouble again."

"Your pleas won't change a thing," the first guard informed her. "Let's get the boy to the dungeon. Hangman, you're expected to be there for the execution first thing in the morning."

"Please, Connor," begged Finnian. "Please don't kill me!" Tears streamed down his cheeks.

Eleanor looked back at Connor, but his face was emotionless. He didn't show a bit of care in his expression. When he spoke, he sounded as if he couldn't care less if the boy should live or die.

"It's my job now," said Connor. "I'm sorry, Finnian, but you made your decision and now you'll have to pay the price. It's always the way. I should know."

"That's right," laughed the guard as they put the boy on the horse with one of them and turned and rode away.

"That poor boy," said Raven, watching them leave.

"That poor boy?" asked Connor. "He had plenty of chances to change and he didn't. He even stole from me. He was warned, but just kept on stealing, and now he'll pay with his life for his choice."

"How can you be so cold-hearted?" snapped Eleanor. "Are you really going to execute the boy tomorrow?"

"Do you think I have a choice?" he retorted. "I don't, Eleanor. I am the executioner now, and you know it. If I don't kill the boy, they'll come after Leoric and make him do it. That is something I can never allow. My brother is already terrified by what he saw yesterday. He is not strong like me. He could never do it."

"Strong? You're strong? Do you really think executing a young boy makes you strong?" asked Eleanor in disgust. "I think it is cowardly not to stand up for what you believe."

His dark eyes bore into her and he looked so dangerous that Eleanor wanted to turn and run. She had never seen Connor with such a stark and cold expression. Still, she stood her ground, waiting for him to respond.

"Do you even know the meaning of *strong*, sweetheart?" he asked her in a cold, cool voice. "Don't bother to answer that, because I will tell you. Strong is having to do what is expected of me when I know that the only things my future holds are pain, anguish, regret, and sorrow," said Connor. "*Strong* is wanting to die, but not taking my own life because I care too damned much what will happen to those I'll leave behind. Strong is pushing aside the man I once was and assuming the position of the most feared and disrespected person of all, being treated worse than lepers because of a decision I made when I was not more than a boy myself.

"It is carrying on in my father's footsteps when I have no desire to walk in his shoes and all I want to do is to run the other way. *Strong* is not questioning why God is punishing me, when all I ever wanted was to honor Him and protect others instead of taking their lives. It is giving up every dream I ever had, and watching the woman I love grieve for me when I am not yet dead. It is taking the path in front of me because I know if I veer off it even the tiniest bit, it will only make things worse for those who mean the most to me in life. That, my dear, is what the hell I mean when I say *strong*."

He turned and stormed away, leaving Eleanor and Raven standing there with their jaws dropped. He entered the house and slammed the door behind him.

"S-should I go after him?" Eleanor asked her cousin, not moving, and not sure anymore what she should do.

"Nay. I think he needs some time alone. Let's get back to the abbey," said Raven, mounting her horse.

"Aye, the children will need us. They'll be very upset."

Eleanor mounted her horse, feeling numb and as if she were in a daze. How could Connor turn so cold so fast? Just yesterday he had seemed so warm and loving and caring. Yesterday, she had hope. Hope that somehow, someway, someday, they would end up together. Now she wasn't so sure she wanted to be with him. He was about to execute Finnian, a boy she'd helped raise and learned to love. Finnian wasn't a bad boy. He was only neglected and crying out for help. For attention. She wished now she could have given him what he'd needed, because a big part of this guilt lay on her shoulders as well.

"This can't be happening," she sobbed, as she rode back to the abbey with Raven. The world was crashing down around her, and sadly, she had no idea how to find a spark of happiness or light in any of this anymore. She couldn't accept that she'd never see Finnian again. Neither could she accept that his death would be by the hand of the man she thought she'd loved.

Mayhap the Connor she once knew and loved no longer existed. The years had been hard on him, and mayhap he'd stopped fighting it and decided to accept his destiny after all.

Sadly, she couldn't accept it, even if he could. And if he went ahead with the execution of this poor boy, then Eleanor didn't want anything to do with Connor ever again.

After a short while, Eleanor and Raven rode through the gates of St. Anne's Abbey, greeted by Lark and the girls.

"There you two are," said Lark. "I've been wondering all morning what happened to you."

Eleanor dismounted and gave the reins to the monk who worked in the stable. Raven did the same.

"Good morning, everyone," said Eleanor, trying to maintain her composure.

"Where is my brother, Connor?" asked Ginevra.

Eleanor wasn't sure how to answer. She noticed that the girl was clutching the rag doll that Lark had bought to give to her own daughter.

"Isn't that the doll you bought for Florie?" asked Eleanor.

"Yes," said Lark. "But Ginevra was upset and I thought she should have it. It helps to comfort her. I'll get another one for my daughter."

"I named the doll Elly, like your name, Lady Eleanor," said Ginevra. Her eyes were sunken in her face, and it looked like she'd been crying.

"Well, it is nice that you have a friend." She bent over and hugged Connor's sister.

"We're her friends, too," said the orphan Margaret. She held on to little Lena's hand.

"Can I have the dolly?" asked Lena, her eyes fixated on the rag doll in Ginevra's hands.

"Nay. Not Elly. She's mine." Ginevra possessively hugged the doll, not wanting to let it go. "She's never going to leave me, the way my mother and father have."

"But I want to play with her," said Lena, pouting.

"Lena, you and Margaret have your own dolls that I gave you," Eleanor gently reminded the girl. "Perhaps your dolls can make friends with Elly. Then you can all play together."

"All right," said Lena. "Ginevra, do you want to see my dolly?"

Ginevra's eyes flashed over to Eleanor. She continued to hug the doll, looking very scared. "I think I have to go home," said Ginevra.

"Oh, shall I go get Alaric and Leoric if they're all leavin'?" asked Lark.

"Nay. Not yet," said Eleanor. "Ginevra, you're going to stay here for another day, so why don't you go with the girls and they'll show you their dolls."

"All right." Ginevra looked up at Lark and held out her hand. "Will you come with us, Lady Lark?"

"Och, well, all right," said Lark with a smile, walking away with the girls.

"Here come Rook and Rose," said Raven. "And Connor's brothers."

Rose walked up carrying little Alaric in her arms. Rook was with her. Leoric followed behind them, his arms wrapped around himself, and his face to the ground. The poor boy really looked traumatized, just like Connor said.

"Where were you two?" asked Rook. "One of the monks told me you rode out at sunrise."

"Yes," said Raven. "I escorted Eleanor to Connor's house."

"Did you say Connor?" Leoric's head snapped up. "Where is he? Is he coming for us?"

"He... he still needs some time alone, so he's back at your house," said Eleanor.

"What's going on?" asked Rose. "Why did you go there?"

"Nothing is going on," said Eleanor with a flash of a smile.

184

"I just thought Connor might need someone to talk to, that's all."

"I saw some of the castle guards ride by just before you arrived," Rook told her. "They seemed to have a prisoner. A boy who only looked to be in his teens."

"Yes," said Eleanor sadly. "It is one of the boys who was an orphan here at the abbey at one time. His name is Finnian."

"Why did they have him with them?" asked Leoric, his arms falling to his sides. "Did he do something bad?"

"They arrested him for stealing and stabbing a guard," Raven explained.

"Oh, no! Is he going to the dungeon?" asked Rose, moving Alaric to her other hip.

"Yes. Yes, he is," she answered, barely able to speak.

"If he's going to the dungeons of Marvane Castle, he'll never walk out of there again," said Rook.

"What do you mean?" asked Leoric, concern showing in his eyes.

"It's known that Lord Sampson is a son-of-a-bitch and doesn't let any of his prisoners live," said Rook.

"Rook, please watch what you say in front of the child." Rose kissed Alaric on his head and the boy clung to her.

"I'm just saying that anyone who is arrested by Sampson is always executed. He's not even giving his prisoners trials anymore."

"Executed?" Leoric's attention shot over to Eleanor. "Is my brother going to have to kill Finnian?"

"Leoric, don't worry about these things," said Eleanor. "Now, why don't we all go get a bite to eat?" The church bells started ringing, announcing that mass was about to begin. "Oh, on second thought, why don't we go to mass? Mayhap we can say a prayer for Finnian."

"Yes, that would be nice," agreed Rose.

As they walked to the church, Leoric ran up next to Eleanor, his arms still hugging tightly around his ribs.

"Connor is the hangman now. He's going to have to kill Finnian and I'm going to have to help him. Isn't that right?"

"Leoric, you don't have to do anything you don't want to do," Eleanor told him, not sure what to say.

"Connor doesn't want to execute anyone. He's never done it by himself, and always fought my father when he tried to get him to pull the lever or swing the blade." Leoric swallowed hard, one hand going to his throat.

"Connor has made his decision, even though I don't agree with it," said Eleanor. "He will be executing Finnian."

"Nay!" cried Leoric. "Lady Eleanor, you have to talk him out of it."

"I tried, but I couldn't do it."

"He can't execute anyone. It's not right. If he does do it, he is going to turn into our father."

Eleanor stopped and put her hands on the boy's shoulders. She didn't want to lie to him and give him false hope. Leoric might be weak like Connor said, but he was still old enough to know the truth and learn to deal with it.

"I'm sorry, Leoric, but I'm afraid that perhaps your brother already has turned into your father, and there is nothing we can do to change that."

WHEN NIGHTFALL CAME and his siblings still hadn't returned to the cottage, Connor knew that Eleanor had kept them at the abbey, and a part of him was glad. Tomorrow would be the first time he would have to do an execution on his own. The thought disgusted and terrified him, but he realized he would have to accept it.

The worst part was that his first hanging would be with a boy he knew. Finnian used to be one of the orphans that Eleanor cared for, too. Connor wasn't sure that Finnian would ever be anything but a thief, but Eleanor seemed to have faith in the boy. She didn't want to see him die, and honestly, neither did Connor. He also didn't want to have to be the one to kill him.

God's toes, his life just kept getting harder and harder. He had paced the floor most of the day in worry. Once again, he was going to have to make a decision that would affect so many other lives in the end.

He had lived years repulsed by his father and his actions. So many times he had judged the man, thinking he was a cruel, cold-hearted bastard to take so many lives. Now he realized he'd misjudged his father, because Connor was in the exact position and knew how awful it felt.

He strapped on his belt with his dagger, seeing his father's executioner sword. His hand shook as he reached out for it. Now that he was the executioner, he was required to carry it. It didn't feel good or right, and he lowered his hand without it. Tomorrow he might need to bring it, but today, he wanted nothing to do with it.

Connor threw his cloak over his shoulders. Leaving the cottage, his eyes fell on the graves of his father and sister. Slowly, he made his way over to them, missing them dearly. He also missed his mother. How many more people in his life were going to die? How much more hell could he take before he went insane?

He walked over to the grave of his father, folding his hands in front of him, praying out loud. "Father," he whispered. "I'm so sorry for your death. I'm also sorry that I despised you for being the hangman. I realize now you never wanted to do it.

But you also didn't want to leave your children as orphans. I understand that and I forgive you."

He wiped a tear from his eye and turned to go, then stopped and walked back to the grave. "I don't want Eleanor to think less of me for what I have to do tomorrow. Then again, I don't want to kill the lad at all. But if I don't, they'll make Leoric do it. You know as well as I, that it would kill him. He's still affected badly by what happened yesterday. Bid the devil, I don't know what to do."

Connor suddenly felt just like his father, needing a drink of whisky. Unfortunately, he had finished it all last night. He hurried to the stable and mounted the horse, making his way to the tavern on the less reputable side of town.

"Connor," said one of the regular whores as he made his way into the tavern. She followed on his heels. "If you're looking for some fun, I'm available."

"Not tonight, Daisy," he told her, taking a seat at the drink board. "Whisky," he told the bar keep. He wasn't sure how long he'd sat there drinking before he recognized a man who sat down next to him. It was Tom the butcher. He looked like hell and as if he'd had more to drink than Connor.

"Tom," said Connor, causing the man to look up.

"Hangman," said Tom, staring down at his drink.

"I don't see you in here too often." Connor picked up his cup and took a drink.

"I had nowhere else to go. The missus is crying and I feel like it's all my fault."

"What happened? What are you talking about?" asked Connor.

"I'm the one who said I didn't want Finnian living with us anymore. If I had shown the boy a little love, or even more attention, mayhap he wouldn't be getting executed tomorrow."

"Oh, that," said Connor, feeling even worse now.

"Can you talk your father out of killing my son?" asked Tom. "I can pay you a little, but I don't have a lot of money since I've had to bribe so many shopkeepers to keep them from turning Finnian over to the authorities. Now none of that seems to have mattered."

"My father is dead," said Connor, finishing off his drink.

"Then... *you* are the one executing my son tomorrow?" Connor saw such sadness in the man's eyes like he'd never seen before.

"Don't think I like this damned job," said Connor, laying money on the drink board and getting up to leave. "Buy Tom a drink. On me," he told the barkeep, throwing down another coin.

He turned to leave, and when he did, Tom's fist labeled him in the jaw. Connor stumbled and had to catch himself on a stool to keep from falling. Blood dripped from the corner of his mouth. He used the back of his hand to wipe it away.

"There's going to be a fight," called out one of the drunks.

Suddenly, everyone in the tavern ran over and crowded around, placing bets on who would win.

"Tom, you know you could be arrested for attacking an executioner." Connor was ready to punch him back, but tried hard to restrain himself.

"Good," said Tom, raising his fists, wanting to fight. "Then you can hang me along with my son tomorrow. You can kill us both. You'd like that, you bastard, wouldn't you?"

It took all Connor's control not to hit the man just to shut him up. But he knew how Tom was feeling. He couldn't blame the man for wanting to kill the one who would take his son's life. Without saying another word, Connor turned and left the tavern, going home to drown in his misery by himself.

CHAPTER 15

Connor dressed for the execution the next morning, having taken an hour just to be able to pick up the sword and wear it on his weapon belt. This all seemed like a dream—a nightmare, and he wished he would wake up so it would all be over.

The door to the cottage burst open and his siblings all rushed in.

"Connor, we're home," cried out Leoric.

"I missed you," said Alaric, running over and clinging to Connor's leg.

"I have a doll to keep me company since I'm so sad," said Ginevra, holding up the doll in front of his face. "I named her Elly after Lady Eleanor."

"I missed you all," said Connor, giving the littles ones a hug. When he went to hug Leoric, his brother stepped back as if he were afraid.

"What's the matter?" asked Connor.

"You're dressed in Father's executioner's robe. And you're wearing his sword. The one used to behead criminals."

"Aye, I am," said Connor. "You know I have to take his place now that he is dead."

"You are going to kill the poor boy Finnian, aren't you?" Hatred poured out from Leoric's eyes.

Connor couldn't bear to see his brother staring at him in this manner. He also wasn't sure how to answer. Now all three of his siblings stared at him, seeming as if they were afraid of him, and that didn't feel good at all. He had always been there to comfort them. Connor was their protector. But now, he wasn't sure what he was anymore.

"All of you know that I have to take Father's place now that he has died," explained Connor. "I don't have a choice. It was part of the deal that saved Father's life."

"But you're going to kill a boy?" asked Ginevra. "That's so sad."

"Yes, I agree, it is awful. However, I have no choice. It is my job now," Connor told them.

They were silent for a moment and then Leoric spoke up.

"Then, I'm coming with you. To assist you," said his brother.

"Nay, Leoric. This isn't for you. You stay here with your siblings." Connor reached out to put his hand on Leoric's shoulder, but his brother slapped his hand away. Once again, Leoric's arms were hugging himself, and he stared at the ground.

"Well, I'd better go," said Connor, grabbing the executioner's hood from the hook on the wall. When he turned around, he stopped. There stood Eleanor in the doorway with the morning sun illuminating her, almost seeming to make her glow.

She wore a bright green velvet gown with a tall gold collar that framed her face. Orange stitched roses were on each shoulder. The sleeves were trimmed in gold and green, and her waist belt had small green beads encompassing it. Her red locks were crowned with a gold metal headpiece that had a small veil attached to it. And around her neck, hanging from a chain, was that damned big gold cross that only reminded him she was an angel and he was naught but the devil.

"Eleanor. What are you doing here?" he asked. Damn, why did she have to look so pretty?

"I brought your siblings home. Of course, I'd be here. Besides, we're joining you at the castle today."

"What?" His head snapped up in surprise. "Nay. You're not bringing my siblings to the hanging. What the hell are you thinking?"

"Why not?" she asked. "If you're the hangman now, they're going to have to get used to seeing you execute people, starting with a boy that isn't much older than Ginevra."

"Don't do this to me," he said under his breath, feeling angry and also a little panicked. How could she even think of subjecting his siblings to something like this? He didn't want his brothers and sister to watch him execute a man—a boy. A damned *boy*. God's eyes this wasn't at all what he wanted.

"Eleanor, we need to leave now if we're going to find seats near the front." Rook came in with Rose at his side. "There will be a crowd today since there is also a festival happening at the castle."

"God's teeth, you're all coming? And you plan to sit up front?" asked Connor, feeling his heart almost beating out of his chest. It was hard enough that this would be his first job, but even worse that everyone he knew would be watching. Especially his family and friends. Eleanor had to be doing this on purpose for some reason, and he despised it.

"Not all of us will be there," said Eleanor. "Lark is staying back at the abbey with Lena and Margaret. The girls are very young and don't want to witness the execution."

"Bid the devil, so are Alaric and Ginevra. I don't want them witnessing it either," said Connor. "Or even Leoric, for that matter."

"You can't stop us, just like we can't stop you from killing Finnian," said Eleanor.

"I know what you're doing, Eleanor, and I don't like it. Can I speak to you outside, please? Alone," he added, sticking the executioner's hood under his arm and walking out the door. When he turned around to talk to her, he realized that everyone had followed him and were standing there listening.

"I don't like this addled game you're playing," he growled. "Now stop it at once."

"It's not a game," she told him, with a serious look upon her face. "This is life, Connor. Or should I say death? Get used to it, because this is the way it is going to be from now on."

"Nay, it's not. I don't want my siblings there to witness this." He raised his hands in the air and when he did, he dropped his hood. Rose, who was standing there as well, bent over and picked it up.

"What is this stain on the hood?" asked Rose, looking closely at the material.

"It looks like blood," said Rook, peeking over her shoulder. "God's eyes, Rose, put it down. Don't touch that."

"Nay, it's not blood. I think it is wine," said Rose, bringing the hood to her nose and taking a sniff.

"That's Father's hood," said Leoric. "He spilled some of the wine on it that Lord Sampson gave him at the execution since his hand was shaking so badly."

"Sampson gave Father wine?" asked Connor, thinking that was an odd thing for him to do. Especially since they hated each other.

"There's an odd odor to the wine stain," said Rose in thought. "I'm sure I've smelled this somewhere before."

"It's the scent of death." Connor snatched the hood away from her, heading over to hitch his horse up to the wagon so he could haul away the dead body after the execution was over. "Stay here, all of you. I repeat, do not follow me to the castle." He finished preparing the wagon and climbed up onto the bench seat, preparing to go.

"Connor, wait." Eleanor ran to him, tears streaming down her cheeks. "Please, don't kill Finnian. There must be some way we can help him instead."

"I wish there were, sweetheart. You know I don't want to do this, but for the life of me, I can't think of a way to get out of this mess."

"That's it!" exclaimed Rose, rushing over to them. "I remember now where I've smelled the scent and I know what it is. It's monkshood." She stood in front of the horse, petting it on its nose.

"I don't really care. Now, move to the side, Rose, or you'll be run over. I need to leave right now," growled Connor.

"Monkshood?" asked Eleanor. "What are you talking about, Rose?"

Rose continued to pet the horse, doing nothing to move, ignoring Connor's command. "I knew I'd smelled that scent before. The one mixed with the wine that was spilled on the executioner's hood, that is. My father used to use it to poison the weeds that got too overpowering in the garden. It's also called wolfsbane. Every part of the plant is poisonous and can be used in many ways to kill something. Or someone."

"Wait a minute. What are you saying?" asked Connor, now taking interest in this.

"I'm saying that I think that wine spilled on the hood had a poisonous plant mixed in it. One that could easily kill a man. Especially a man who is already weak and ill. It wouldn't take much, and the wine disguises the bitter taste."

"So, are you saying that Sampson killed my father?" asked Connor.

"Well, I don't know for sure," said Rose. "But I do smell the herb in that spilled wine, so I think it could be true."

"Father didn't want to drink the wine, but Lord Sampson forced him to do it," said Leoric.

"Good God, Father has been murdered," said Connor. "But how can we prove it?"

"If we had the lord's goblet that the wine was served in, it might still hold traces of the wolfsbane," said Raven.

"Well, we don't have it," said Connor in thought. "By now, Lord Sampson has probably washed off any traces of the poison anyway."

"Nay, he didn't," said Leoric. When Father drank from it, he dropped the cup and it rolled into the blood of the... beheaded man. Lord Sampson told me he didn't want the goblet back and that I had to bury it with the body. He also said if I stole the cup, he'd have me beheaded for taking it."

"So, what did you do?" asked Rose.

"I buried it, just like he told me to do. With the body," said Leoric. "I was frightened that he might behead me if I didn't."

"Brother, do you remember where you buried that body?" asked Connor, finding a sudden spark of hope.

"I do," said Leoric. "It's in the prisoner's graveyard. Connor, please don't tell me you are going to make me dig it up." He held his hands over his stomach as if the idea made him nauseous.

"If we can find that goblet, we'll have the proof we need that Father was murdered. I am sure we can link the murder to Sampson," said Connor.

"Oh, Connor, that would be great," said Eleanor. "And what about Finnian?"

"Well, in the commotion of the festival, I might be able to

free Finnian. However, I can't do that and dig up the cup too," said Connor.

"I'll dig it up," offered Rook. "Leave that part to me."

"Nay. You're a noble," said Connor. "I can't ask you to do that."

"If it'll help you and your family and free that poor boy, I'll do whatever it takes." Rook surprised him by saying this, since his participation in such a scheme was the last thing that Connor ever expected.

"If I free Finnian, he's going to have to hide until this is all over," Connor pointed out. "Also, things might not go as planned and I don't want the guards coming after my siblings because of it. We'll have to find a place to hide them until this is all over as well."

"Your siblings can stay at Blake Castle with me," offered Raven.

"Nay, Sister," said Rook with a scowl on his face. "That would put Father and Mother in danger."

"Well, we have to do something to help them," said Raven.

"I agree. We have to do something to help them," echoed Rose.

"Fine," said Rook with a sigh. Connor, your siblings will stay with Rose and me at Rookrose Manor."

"Truly?" asked Eleanor. "You would do that, Cousin?"

"Unless you want to hide them at the abbey," suggested Rook.

"Nay." Eleanor shook her head. "That is the first place Sampson would look. Besides, I can't put all the nuns in that dangerous position. If the abbess found out about it, she'd probably turn you all in by herself."

"Then Rookrose it is," said Rose with a smile, walking over and taking her husband's arm.

"I'll try to free Finnian. Where should I send him afterwards?" asked Connor.

"I'll be there," said Eleanor. "I can help sneak him out of the dungeon while Rook digs up the cup."

"Nay," objected Connor. "I have reason to be in the dungeon, you don't. Besides, I don't want you anywhere near that awful place. And I'll tell you again that I don't want my siblings there either."

Eleanor let out a sigh. "I'll make sure Alaric and Ginevra spend the day at the abbey, but there is nothing you can say that will keep me away from Marvane Castle today, Connor. I feel responsible for Finnian and won't abandon him."

"Fair enough," mumbled Connor.

"Connor, I don't mind helping out, but I need to know exactly where to find the goblet," said Rook. "I can't be digging blindly."

"I'll go with you and show you exactly where I buried it," said Leoric, standing taller and looking more confident now.

"Leoric, are you sure?" asked Connor. "No one expects you to do this."

"I want to help," said Leoric. "After all, if you were willing to take Father's place as hangman to keep me from having to be the executioner, then this is the least I can do to show you how much that means to me."

"Then let's go," said Connor. "The festival is already in progress, and we have no time to waste."

CHAPTER 16

"Let me in. I'm here to get the prisoner," said Connor, wearing his executioner's attire, standing at the door leading to the dungeon.

"You're here already?" asked the guard. "The execution isn't scheduled until later today. Lord Sampson wants to make sure the crowds are excited and drinking plenty before it happens."

"Well, he changed his mind," lied Connor. "Lord Sampson wants it done earlier. Let me in, I say."

"All right, all right," grumbled the guard, stepping aside and opening the door that led down to the dungeon. Connor had left his brother and Rook outside the castle walls at the prisoners' graveyard to dig up the cup. Rose and Raven were waiting at the far side of the gallows with the wagon from the abbey. The plan was that Connor would lead the boy to them, and then he'd disappear into the crowd. Finnian would hide in the back of the wagon and ride right out the gates without anyone knowing it. Connor would wait long enough before he made the announcement that Finnian had escaped.

Connor wasn't sure what Eleanor was planning on doing, but she'd told him right before they left that she'd keep an eye on Lord Sampson.

He felt extremely nervous about this plan. He was worried, not for himself, but for the others. If even one little thing went wrong, the whole plan could fall apart. Connor might end up having to kill Finnian after all, and he really hoped he wouldn't have to do that.

Anger grew within him with every step he took. He kept thinking how his poor father was poisoned by Lord Sampson. He figured it was because his father took too many swings of the sword to do his last beheading. Executions that went awry and got too messy always angered the nobles because they wanted clean, fast kills. Sampson most likely wanted to punish his father for that. But what kind of man reverts to using poison and actually killing the hangman? He could have just refused to pay him and that would have hurt enough. Connor had the feeling what Sampson did was with a personal vendetta. He was still angry that Connor's father had killed his brother and wanted revenge.

"I'm here for the prisoner. The one called Finnian," Connor told the guard outside the cells.

"Already?" asked the man, taking a swig of wine from a bottle.

"Yes. I was told to come get him and bring him to the gallows."

"I don't believe you, hangman," said the guard. "And I don't let no one in unless I hear the order from Lord Sampson's mouth personally. Go away and come back later." He raised the bottle and took another swig.

Connor looked back over his shoulder, making sure he wasn't being followed. "I don't have time for this," he mumbled, grabbing the bottle from the guard and hitting him hard over the head. The bottle shattered, the guard's eyes rolled back, and he collapsed at Connor's feet.

"Now, that's better," said Connor, reaching down and unclasping the ring of keys from the man's belt. He hurriedly let himself into the dungeon, finding Finnian and unlocking his cell door. "Let's go. And keep quiet about it, we don't want to alert the guards," said Connor with a shake of his head.

Finnian was sitting on the floor with his head down. When he saw Connor, he jumped up, backing away, holding out his hands.

"Nay! Don't take me to the gallows, hangman. I don't want to die."

"Quiet down," grunted Connor. "I'm here to rescue you, not execute you. However, if you don't work with me, you might just end up on the gallows after all."

"Do you mean that? You're not going to kill me?" he asked, still not believing Connor. "You're helping me to escape?"

Connor lowered his hood and showed the boy his face. "I'm doing this for Lady Eleanor, Finnian. She is very fond of you for some reason, although I can't really see why. Now don't make this harder than it has to be. I'm putting my neck on the line for you, even though, unless you've forgotten, you stole from me as well."

"Oh, so you are Lady Eleanor's friend? Or are you her lover?"

That comment made Connor want to wring the boy's neck.

"Keep up with questions like that and I might just leave you here after all. Now shut up and do as I say. We have one chance at this, and if you mess up, we both might be killed because of it."

"I'll listen. I promise I will," said the boy, running to the open cell door. "Just tell me what to do and I'll do it."

"Well, for starters, you'd better say a silent prayer."

"Pray? What for?"

"Because I have a bad feeling about this and I think we're going to need all the prayers we can get."

THE CROWDS WERE GATHERING for the festival at the castle, and Eleanor wished Connor would hurry and free Finnian because it was getting riskier each moment they waited. The more people that arrived meant more of them that they would have to avoid to try to sneak Finnian out of here. Afterwards, Connor was going to have to make himself scarce until after Rook and Leoric dug up the goblet. She prayed they could prove that Lord Sampson murdered Connor's father since she was sure now that it was true. It was their only hope of ever getting Connor out of the position of being the hangman. She wasn't sure yet just exactly how they'd do that, but she hoped she'd think of something before the time came.

She looked over and motioned to Raven and Rose who were sitting in the wagon they had brought from the abbey. They were both dressed like nuns and were waiting for Finnian. After all, no one would stop a nun or suspect they would do anything deceptive at all.

"Lady Eleanor, so nice to see you here at my festival."

She whirled around and groaned inwardly when she saw Lord Sampson approaching with his entourage of guards all around him.

"Lord Sampson," she said with a curtsy. To think she grew up here and had looked up to the man at one time made her want to retch.

"I've invited everyone to the grand festival. And in case you haven't heard, the main event is the hanging of that young thief," he said with a chuckle, as if the thought of killing a boy amused him. "I've scheduled it for this afternoon. I figured the bigger the crowd, the better. The gallows are always a big draw. What fun."

"Fun? I don't understand how you can think killing anyone, let alone a young boy, is fun!"

"He's not a boy. He's a young man. It's a shame he won't live long enough to even grow a beard."

That made his guards laugh, and caused Eleanor's stomach to tighten.

"If you'll excuse me," she said, trying to walk away, but Sampson grabbed her arm and pulled her along with him.

"You'll stay by me. I want to see your expression when your past betrothed is the one to hang that pitiful orphan boy."

Her head jerked upward. "Why would you think Connor would be the one doing the execution? After all, his father always does it."

"Well, how the hell is the man going to pull the lever when he's dead?" He laughed again.

"How do you know he's dead? Who told you?"

He stopped laughing and looked over to one of his guards.

"I told him," said the guard.

"And how did you know?" asked Eleanor.

"I was at the hangman's house earlier and his son told me."

"That's a lie. I was there when the guards arrived and remember the guards clearly. You were not one of them."

"My guards report everything to me. They all know what is going on," said Sampson, making Eleanor realize it probably was true. "Besides, what does it matter?" asked Sampson. "Let's go closer to the gallows while we wait. The anticipation is making me anxious."

Eleanor saw Connor and Finnian sneaking through the crowd and Sampson was headed right toward them.

"Lord Sampson," she called out, stopping him is his tracks.

"What is it?" He turned back to look at her, thankfully not seeing Finnian getting into the back of the wagon.

"I was... wondering. I mean, what other things will be happening today? At the festival?"

Raven drove the wagon right past them, directly behind Sampson. He didn't even look. She kept the man's attention until from the corners of her eyes she saw the wagon passing through the main gate.

"You'll just have to wait and find out."

A serving wench walked by holding a tray of wooden goblets filled with wine.

"Wait," said Sampson, taking two goblets and handing one of them to Eleanor, keeping the other for himself. "Lady Eleanor, I see you haven't yet taken a husband. Why is that?"

"I'm not interested in getting married."

"Well, you have been living at the abbey for years now, yet you have not taken any vows. Why is this?"

"I-I'm not planning on becoming a nun. I just take care of the orphans," she told him, lifting the cup to her mouth and then stopping, remembering that this man liked to poison people. She didn't want to take a chance. "One of those orphans is the boy I've place with a family. The same one you have condemned to death."

"I see." He took a sip of wine, watching her over the rim of his goblet. That told her the wine wasn't poisoned, but still she didn't want to chance it.

When he turned to talk to his guard, she dumped the wine behind her when she pretended to cough. Then when he turned back around, she pretended to have drunk it all, plopping the cup down on the tray of a passing servant.

"I have invited your parents to the festival today. I hadn't planned on it, but I think mayhap I'll make an alliance with your father that includes marrying you."

"What?" she gasped. Hearing this making her entire body shake.

He pulled her to him, running his beefy hand over the side of her cheek. "After all, a prize like you shouldn't be wasted."

Eleanor wanted to bite him, spit on him, and tell him off. But she needed to give Connor time to get out of here as well. Until they had that goblet, he couldn't be seen.

"What's the matter?" asked Sampson. "You're not still pining for that stupid hangman, are you? You know you can never marry him."

"And neither will I ever marry *you*! Remember, my father was good friends with Wensel Wyland, the man you wanted to behead. The man you are responsible for turning into the hangman." She could no longer hold back her anger.

"I had nothing to do with that hangman crap. If it were up to me, he would have died that day for killing my brother."

He held her wrist tightly and she struggled to get loose. That's when she noticed Connor stopping and looking over at them. She prayed he would keep on going, but like she knew he would do, he beelined it over to them instead.

"Here comes the hangman, my lord," one of the guards informed him.

"Good," said Sampson with a chuckle. "I can't wait to see his face when he finds out I'm marrying his past betrothed."

"My parents would never agree to me marrying you," said Eleanor, still struggling to get out of his hold.

"Oh, never mind. You are too feisty of a wench. You'll be too much trouble. I don't think I want you in my bed after all."

"Is there a problem here?" asked Connor, walking up next to Eleanor.

"Nay, everything is fine," said Eleanor, trying to motion to Connor with her eyes to get the heck out of there.

"The only problem, Executioner, is that you should be

preparing for the hanging," said Sampson. "What are you doing over here speaking to me like that? Get back by the gallows where you belong. No one wants you near them."

"My lord, the prisoner has escaped," yelled the prison guard, rubbing his head and running out into the courtyard. "The hangman helped him escape."

"What?" asked Sampson, releasing Eleanor. Connor grabbed her and started running. "Get them!" shouted the lord of the castle.

"Connor, what are you doing?" Eleanor looked up at him in surprise. "This wasn't part of the plan."

"I'm trying to save you," he said, pushing his way through the crowd, pulling her along with him.

"Everything is ruined now. Lord Sampson knows you helped Finnian escape."

"It doesn't matter. The guard I knocked over the head was going to tell him sooner or later. Let's get the hell out of here." He ran back to get his horse, but one of the castle guards was already there. They turned and ran the other way, only to bump into two more guards coming at them with their weapons drawn. And when they turned once more, they crashed right into Lord Sampson. The edge of the man's blade rested under Connor's chin.

"Bad move, fool," spat Sampson. "Because even without the boy, one way or another I am going to have a hanging today."

"The boy didn't deserve to die," said Connor.

"Mayhap now you'll have to die in his place."

"Nay!" screamed Eleanor. "Leave him be. He did nothing wrong."

"I'm not afraid to die," said Connor. "But who is going to kill me? You? I don't believe you are brave enough to do it. Unless you plan to poison me, just like you did to my father."

"Connor, no," said Eleanor under her breath, not wanting him to say that. Not yet. Now that Sampson realized they knew his secret, he would never let either of them go. He wouldn't want to be exposed for murdering a man.

"Shall we take him away?" asked the guards, holding Connor by his arms.

"Nay, the fool is right about one thing. There would be no one to pull the lever since he's the damned hangman."

"What does that mean?" asked one of his men.

"It means, I have to find someone else to execute instead." His eyes roamed over to Eleanor. "Mayhap her."

"Nay!" screamed Connor.

"My lord? You want to kill a lady?" asked the guard. "What did she do?"

"She deceived me. She is part of this plot helping prisoners escape, and for that the wench should be punished." He laughed heartily now. "Won't this be amusing? The hangman will kill her while we all watch him take the life of the woman he was once supposed to marry."

"Nay! Leave me alone," cried Eleanor as the guards grabbed her and dragged her to the gallows.

"You bastard," shouted Connor. "I would never hurt a hair on her head. I love Eleanor and I will not let you or anyone kill her."

"Indeed?" asked Sampson, laughing once again.

"Remember, she is the daughter of the Lord Warden. Do you really think you will get away with this?" shouted Connor.

"Oh, that's right," said Sampson, his smile turning into a frown. "Perhaps that won't work. Release her," he called out to his guards. He looked directly at Connor. "Mayhap, instead, I'll just have to kill that stupid brother of yours instead."

"What?" gasped Connor.

"Bring him out!" Sampson shouted to his guards.

The guards dragged Leoric through the crowd, bringing him up to the gallows.

"Nay! Leave him alone," yelled Connor. "Isn't it bad enough that you already scarred him for life, making him think it was his fault our father died when it was really *you* who murdered him?"

"Such accusations hold no power here," said Sampson. "You have no proof, hangman. This boy was caught digging up corpses in the prisoners' field and that is not allowed. There was another with him, but he escaped. Until we find him, this one will be punished. So you see, even though you helped the prisoner escape, I'll still have my hanging after all. And you will be the one to do it."

Connor suddenly realized that the man was right. They had no proof now that Sampson murdered his father. Without that blasted goblet, they would never be able to prove a damned thing. His only hope now was that Rook would be able to sneak back and find the goblet.

"Let go of me, you idiots—don't you know who I am?"

Connor's heart sank when he heard the voice of Rook. He looked up to see Rook struggling against half a dozen guards as well. He realized now that they were doomed. Every damned one of them.

"You kill Lord Rook, and Lord Blake will have your head," Connor told Sampson.

"I'm not going to have him killed, you fool," said Sampson. "I'm just detaining him until you hang your brother. You see, no one cares about the brother of a hangman. This is one execution that the crowd will welcome. Guards, hold on to Lord Rook and Lady Eleanor until the hangman has done his job."

Eleanor was brought down from the gallows, and two guards dragged Leoric up the stairs instead. They quickly put the noose around Leoric's neck. His hands were tied behind him.

"Do it, hangman. The crowd is waiting and came for a killing," said Sampson. "We don't want to disappoint them."

"Nay, I won't do it. Leoric did nothing to you. There is no reason to kill him."

"He did nothing, but *you* certainly did. You let my prisoner go free, and you really shouldn't have done that. Now, your brother will take the boy's place, and it is all because of you."

"Hang him, hang him," shouted the crowd. Men with full tankards of ale pushed to the front to get a good view. It made Connor so angry.

Leoric looked back at Connor, fear showing in his eyes. His entire body shook and his teeth chattered in fear. The guard started to put a bag over his brother's head but Connor stopped him.

"Nay, don't! Get away from him," he told the guard.

"Oh, that's right, it's the hangman's job to do this." The guard threw the bag to the floor, but left Leoric with the noose around his neck and walked over to the side. Lord Sampson walked over to the stairs that led up to the gallows.

"Do it, hangman. And hurry up about it. I have other festivities planned today that I want to get to."

The crowd became unruly. It seemed as if Sampson and his men had convinced them that Connor had been wrong in helping a prisoner escape. They wanted to see someone punished for this, and they cared naught about the family of a hangman.

Connor walked slowly to his brother, bending down and picking up the bag. He looked out at the crowd, feeling the hatred, wanting nothing more than to be away from here and never being in this position again. Once again, Connor's decision was going to hurt his family.

"Nay," he called out to the crowd. "I will not kill my brother today or ever. He did nothing wrong. The one who should be punished for murder is right there." He turned and pointed to where Lord Sampson had been standing at the foot of the stairs but he was gone.

"Never mind, hangman. I'll do it myself."

Connor's head jerked around to see Lord Sampson with his hand on the lever to the drop floor. Connor realized the noose was still around his brother's neck, and poor Leoric's hands were tied. As if in slow motion, Connor watched in horror as Lord Sampson yanked the lever to release the drop floor.

The sound of the floor opening beneath his brother's feet echoed like an explosion in Connor's head. His brother's scared eyes looked out at Connor as his body started to fall through the floor, taking Leoric to his death.

CHAPTER 17

Eleanor screamed when she realized what she was witnessing, not able to believe that Lord Sampson had just pulled the lever to send Connor's brother to his death.

She expected to see the poor boy's body dangling from the gallows, but instead, in one motion, Connor grabbed his brother with one arm, pulling his sword from his side and chopping the rope that held the noose. They both lost their balance and Eleanor screamed again as Connor and Leoric fell through the floor, landing with a loud thump under the gallows.

She stepped on one guard's toe and kneed another in the groin, breaking free and running over to Connor and his brother. She heard a commotion behind her and realized that Rook had also broken free and was fighting off several guards at once with his sword.

"Connor! Leoric! Are you all right?" Eleanor threw herself to the ground, hoping they were not dead.

"A little bruised but no worse for wear." Connor used his

dagger to cut the ropes binding Leoric's hands. "Are you all right, Brother?"

"Aye," said Leoric, rubbing his wrists. "That was a little close. And now I know what it feels like to be on the other end of the noose. I don't like it and never want to experience that again."

"Don't worry, you won't have to because we are no longer going to be executioners," Connor told him.

"We're not?" asked Leoric in confusion. "Connor, Rook and I didn't have a chance to dig up the goblet before Sampson stopped us. We have no proof that our father was murdered."

"Are you coming out of there anytime soon?" asked Rook, looking over his shoulder as he continued to fight the guards. "I could use a little help out here."

"Let's go," said Connor, helping his brother to his feet.

"Don't try to leave because there is no escaping this," Sampson called down to them from up above, looking through the open floor.

"That's where you're wrong, Lord Sampson," came a deep voice from the courtyard. "Everyone, quiet down. Quiet, I say."

"Put down your weapons," came another man's voice. "There will be no more fighting here today."

Eleanor looked up to see her father, as well as her Uncle Corbett. They each had a small entourage of their own soldiers with them.

"What is the meaning of this?" screamed Sampson, still standing on the gallows.

The crowd moved to the sides, allowing the Lord Warden and his men, as well as Lord Corbett and his men, to rule the courtyard.

"Are you all right, Eleanor?" asked Connor, putting his arm around her.

"Yes. Yes, I'm not hurt," she told him, wondering what was going to happen now.

"You have no right to barge into my courtyard as if you owned it, and order my guards to drop their weapons," yelled Sampson.

"The Lord Warden has every right, and by permission granted to him by the King himself, he can do whatever the hell he wants here," said Lord Corbett.

"Well, what is it you want?" asked Sampson.

"Father," said Eleanor, breaking away from Connor and running over to him. "Lord Sampson has murdered Connor's father."

"That is a lie," snapped Sampson, speaking loudly and holding out his arms, still standing atop the gallows as if he were in a play. "You have no proof to back up these accusations."

"Actually, we do," said a woman. Raven walked out of the crowd with Rose. They were still dressed as nuns.

"What? Two nuns are going to speak against me? This is ridiculous," said Sampson.

"Who said we were nuns?" Rose lowered her hood and held up a dirty metal goblet. "This is the goblet he used to poison Wensel Wyland, the last hangman. Lord Sampson tried to stop my husband and Connor's brother from digging it up, but Raven and I had the pleasure of carrying out the task ourselves."

The crowd talked to each other in soft voices.

"You have a goblet? So what? That proves nothing," said Sampson, still laughing.

"This is the goblet you used to poison Connor's father. Admit it," said Raven.

"Where did you get that?" asked Sampson, squinting his eyes, suddenly seeming worried.

"You told Leoric to bury it with the dead man, and we retrieved it," Raven answered.

"He was trying to hide the evidence," Connor pointed out. He and Leoric joined the others.

"That's it! That's the cup he used to poison Father." Leoric pushed his way over to Rose and Raven to inspect it closer.

"You are going to believe his word over mine? I'm a noble. He's just the son of the hangman." Sampson still didn't seem overly concerned.

"Wine you forced my father to drink, spilled from this goblet on to my father's hood the day of the last beheading," said Connor. "This is that same hood." Connor removed his hood and held it up for all to see.

"The scent of the poisonous herb, wolfsbane can be smelled on the hood as well as the goblet," Rose told them.

"Nonsense. I don't know what you are talking about," said Sampson.

"It's true! Father died before I even got him home that day," cried Leoric.

"Nay. That's not true," Sampson still protested.

"Is it really?" Connor looked over to his brother. "Leoric, do you recognize any of these people as being the same ones that were here the day of the beheading?"

Leoric craned his neck, looking over the guards and people in the crowd. "I do," he answered. "Actually, I recognize lots of them."

"Who are they? Can you point one out to us?" asked Lord Corbett.

"Well, I remember that lady," said Leoric, pointing to one of the ladies of the castle. "She was actually kind to me. She stood right in the front and saw everything the day of the beheading."

"Lady Stephanie, you are a well-respected noblewoman,"

said Eleanor's father, Garret Blackmore, recognizing her as well. "Can you tell me if this is Lord Sampson's goblet? Come here and take a good look, please."

The woman walked over, taking a look at the goblet and nodding. "Yes, Lord Warden, it is. My husband gave it to him last year." Her husband was right behind her and acknowledged the fact as well.

"So, that still proves nothing other than it is my goblet." Sampson didn't seem so confident anymore.

"Did you see Lord Sampson give wine in this goblet to the hangman the day of the beheading?" asked Lord Corbett.

"Well, I think so," said the woman. "But I can't be sure."

"I can. I saw it," spoke up a priest from the village. "Lord Sampson came to me that morning asking for the darkest red wine I had. I gave it to him and saw him later forcing that poor hangman to drink it. The executioner was coughing and didn't even want it, but was forced to drink it."

"I can vouch that the herb I smell on both the hood and goblet is poisonous," said Rose.

"Who the hell are you?" snapped Sampson.

"That is my wife, Lady Rose," said Rook. "She was a gardener and knows all there is about any kind of herb."

"You are going to take a gardener's word over mine now?" spat Sampson, shaking his head and blowing air from his mouth. "That won't hold up in any court."

"He sent his guard to my shop that morning to buy wolfsbane," said a man, breaking through the crowd.

"And who are you?" asked Garrett.

"I am the apothecary and also the healer of the village," said an older man. "I only carry that herb to help control pests that eat all the crops. I didn't want to sell it to him but I was forced to do it."

"I see," said Garrett. "Lord Sampson, I am Lord Warden of the Barons of the Cinque Ports. As you know, I have the authority to put you under arrest for the murder of Wensel Wyland, and that is exactly what I am going to do. Seize him," commanded Garrett. His guards rushed up to the gallows to get Lord Sampson. "I also heard what just went on here minutes ago, and I cannot condone it. My daughter as well as a boy were mistreated and threatened. You are condemned to death, Lord Sampson for all your crimes. And since you are a noble, as is proper, you will die by beheading. Will you do the honors, Connor?"

"Nay!" screamed Sampson, now being held by the Lord Warden's guards. "I demand a trial."

"There is no need to waste time with a trial," said Garrett. "You didn't allow Sir Wensel that courtesy, and neither will I allow it to you. I have enough witnesses here and enough information to sidestep a trial and go directly to the execution. Hangman, your services are needed please."

Connor looked over to the gallows where Lord Sampson already had his hands tied behind his back. The guards had closed the trap door and pushed Sampson down to his knees. The stump used for beheadings was brought over and placed in front of him.

As much as Connor would love to kill the man for murdering his father, he couldn't bring himself to do it. Would it really make him any better than Sampson if he killed him out of anger, wanting revenge? Then again, it was Connor's job now, and he had to do it.

"With all due respect, Lord Warden," said Connor. "I am afraid I cannot execute Lord Sampson."

"Why the hell not?" shouted Rook. "God's eyes, Connor, the man murdered your father and almost made you kill your own brother. What are you saying?"

"I know, and I hate him more than anyone for what he did to not only my father, but to my entire family," said Connor.

"Well your father started all this when he killed my brother!" shouted Sampson. "It was only fair that I pay back the favor. I had no choice but to kill him. He deserved it."

"And there is the confession I was looking for. Thank you," said the Lord Warden. "Now, it is complete, and you have sealed your own fate, Lord Sampson."

"Wait a second," said Connor, raising a hand in the air. "I know my father was wrong in what he did. He murdered a man. A nobleman. And as much as it pains me having to say this, my father deserved to die for his crime."

"Connor, what are you doing? What are you saying?" asked Eleanor.

"Hold on, sweetheart," he said. "Let me finish. I have lived in hell these past five years, and just lived through hell again when those I loved were threatened and my brother was almost executed. It's not a good feeling to lose anyone. Especially a brother. Lord Sampson, I want to apologize for my father's crime of killing your brother. I honestly wish that it had never happened."

"That's just fine, hangman, but it doesn't bring him back," yelled Sampson.

"No, sadly, it doesn't," agreed Connor. "And neither will my father be brought back to life after your hand in his death."

"I'm not apologizing for killing your father, if that is what you're waiting for. He deserved to die just like you said. I'm not the least bit sorry for killing him."

"Kill him, kill him," shouted the crowd, siding with Connor now and wanting to do away with Lord Sampson.

"God's eyes, Connor, why are you stalling?" complained Rook. "The man deserves to die. Follow the Lord Warden's orders. Stop all this talking and execute him! It is your job now."

"Nay, beheading is too good for the likes of him," said Connor.

"Then would you prefer hanging, or to have him drawn and quartered?" asked Eleanor's father. "You are the hangman and I will leave the decision of how he'll die up to you."

"Thank you," said Connor. "But I actually don't want him to be killed at all."

"You don't?" asked Garrett. "I don't understand. Why not?"

"Connor, what are you saying?" gasped Eleanor. "This man has ruined your life!"

"That's right, he has," said Connor. "And that is why instead of killing him, I ask you, Lord Warden to spare his life instead."

"Spare his life? That makes no sense. Connor you are mad," shouted Rook.

"Nay, I'm not. I want Lord Sampson to know what my father and my entire family had to live through. I want him to feel the loss and feel the pain. I'd like him to make the same trade for his life that my father made for his."

"Oh, I see what you're doing," said Eleanor with a smile.

"I want Lord Sampson's life spared, but in return he will have to agree to take over the position of hangman from now on," continued Connor. "Therefore, I will be freed from the position of executioner and my family will be freed as well."

"What?" asked Sampson, shaking his head. "Nay, I won't do it. Cut off my head right now, because I would prefer that to the humility of taking the position of hangman."

"Lord Warden, this is your decision," said Corbett.

Garrett looked over to Eleanor. "Daughter, what do you want me to do?"

"Nay, please don't put her in that position," interrupted

Connor. "I lived through that agony and don't wish it on anyone. Especially such a beautiful, wonderful woman as Eleanor. This decision is not hers to make."

"You are absolutely right," said Garrett with a nod. "I think it is a fair punishment for this man's crimes. Usually, the convicted has a choice whether or not to accept being executioner. But in this case, I am making the decision for him. Lord Sampson, by the powers granted to me by the King, I declare that from this day on, you will assume the position of hangman, thereby relieving Connor Wyland and his family from any further obligations." The crowd gasped and mumbled comments. "You will from this moment on, lose your title, your castle, your lands and money, and also all respect."

"Oh, thank you, Father," said Eleanor, running to him and giving him a kiss on the cheek and a big hug.

"Wait, that's not all," said Garrett. "I am also granting Connor and his family the right to reclaim their titles. The Wyland family will no longer be treated poorly and disrespected. Everyone will treat them just like any other nobles from this day forward, forgetting about what happened in the past. Also, Connor Wyland will continue with his training of squire where he left off five years ago, and someday become a knight, just like the original plan."

"I will offer to personally train Connor at Blake Castle," offered Lord Corbett.

These decisions made the crowd go wild. Connor was dumbstruck, not even knowing what to say. He thought at first that he might be dreaming it all, until Eleanor ran to his side and grabbed him by the arm.

"Connor, isn't this wonderful? Connor, say something, please. Did you hear my father? You are free from being a hangman and will be able to become a knight someday, just like you've always wanted."

"Yes. Thank you," said Connor. "Thank you, Lord Warden and Lord Blake. I am grateful for everything. This is a dream come true. However, Lord Warden, there is one more thing I would like restored, if it isn't too bold of me to ask."

"What is it you want?" asked Garrett.

"Eleanor and I were once betrothed."

"True." Garrett nodded but didn't say more.

"What I would really like is your daughter Lady Eleanor's hand in marriage. If she'll have me," said Connor taking her hand and squeezing it in his. "I hope she'll still want me, even though I wouldn't blame her if she didn't."

"Oh, yes, I do want to marry you, Connor. Father, please say yes," begged Eleanor. "That is all I ever wanted. I love Connor and want to be his wife."

"And I love Eleanor and want to be her husband," added Connor. "I promise I'll be the best husband, and someday the best knight I can be. I realize I have nothing to offer her, and for that I am sorry. I have nothing to offer, that is, but my love."

"You were once betrothed to my daughter when I made an alliance with your father, but now he is gone," said Garrett. "I thought it was a good idea then, but things have changed, I'm afraid. It's not so easy to agree to let my only daughter marry someone who used to be a hangman and who has no castle to protect her or money to pamper her the way I think she should be."

"Garrett," said Eleanor's mother, Echo, walking to the front of the crowd. Connor hadn't even known she was there. She spoke in a soft voice so only those standing right there could hear her. "How can you say that after you just told everyone to respect Connor and treat him the same as any noble?" asked Lady Echo. She was a beautiful woman with dark hair and dark eyes. She was Lord Corbett's sister.

"That's true," said Corbett. "At one time my sister was a

pirate, yet you loved her and didn't judge her then. Give Eleanor and Connor the same chance that you had."

"They're in love, dear," said Echo, taking her husband's hand. "Just like us. Nothing but love really matters."

"Father, Connor never actually killed anyone, if that will change your decision. He just assisted his father with the executions," explained Eleanor.

"That's right," agreed Connor. "I never actually pulled the lever or swung the blade to end a prisoner's life."

"Well, it doesn't make a difference if he did or didn't kill a single person," said Garrett. "I have made my decision and will stick by it."

Connor thought this meant he refused to let him marry Eleanor, but his next words proved him wrong.

"I agree that you two should be married," said Garrett. "And I thank my wife for pointing out to me that love between two people is so important. Not, of course, that I believe it is all that matters, but it does hold a good weight when it comes to making decisions."

"Thank you, Husband," said Echo, flashing him a smile.

"Well, my dear wife," Garrett said softly. "I know if I don't agree to the marriage, Eleanor will end up living in the damned abbey forever and probably become a nun. I want grandchildren," said Garrett with a chuckle. "At least this way, I might actually have some."

"Thank you, Lord Warden. And I promise you, I will do my best to give you many grandchildren," said Connor, leaning over and kissing Eleanor on the mouth.

Then it is done," said Garrett, causing the crowd to cheer. "My daughter, Lady Eleanor of Hythe, will marry Lord Connor Wyland at the earliest convenience."

"What do you say, Connor? Isn't this exciting?" asked Eleanor, crying tears of joy.

"I can hardly believe it," he told her, bending over and kissing her once again. "I am afraid I will wake up and find out this is all naught but a dream."

"It is a dream," she told him. "A dream come true. Now, we can finally be together, forever, as husband and wife."

CHAPTER 18

A WEEK LATER, BLAKE CASTLE, DEVON

Today, the wedding was scheduled to take place at Blake Castle in Devon, where Connor had been made squire to Lord Corbett Blake. His training to become a knight would continue as soon as Connor and Eleanor married, making their permanent home here, for now.

Eleanor stood nervously in the solar, waiting for her father to arrive to escort her to the great hall, where the wedding would commence. Lark, Rose, and Raven were with her.

"I'm nervous," admitted Eleanor as Lark finished plaiting her hair. Florie, Lark's daughter, handed Lark wildflowers that Lark wove into the plaiting.

"Why are ye nervous?" asked Lark. "I thought ye wanted to marry Connor."

"Aye," agreed Rose. "There is nothing to be afraid of. After all, your marriage is accepted by all. Mine was a different story altogether."

"I know that, but still, I've waited for this for so long," said Eleanor. "Remember, I was betrothed as a child, so I had more time to think about getting married than the rest of you."

"And that is why you should be more at ease with marriage than the rest of us, too." Raven walked over, covering Eleanor's head with a thin veil, pinning it in place.

"I'm nervous too," said Florie.

"You?" asked Eleanor with a giggle. "Whatever for?"

"Because, I have to throw down the rose petals. What if I do it wrong?" Florie got up and picked up her basket, taking a handful of petals and tossing them high in the air.

"No' so many at once or ye'll run out before ye get to the priest," said Lark, hurrying over to help her young daughter pick up the petals and place them back into the basket.

There came a quick knock at the door. Since Lark was there, she opened it.

"Robin!" she exclaimed, giving the man a hug.

Eleanor looked over to see their cousin Robin, surprised he had showed up for the wedding.

"Robin. What are you doing here?" asked Eleanor. "I figured you'd be busy with that new castle of yours."

"Never too busy to attend the wedding of one of my cousins," said Robin. "I'm here to take you to your father who is waiting outside the great hall. Everyone is here, including the priest."

"Why didn't my father come to get me himself?" asked Eleanor.

"He said he wanted to stay there to talk with the other nobles," said Robin. "Honestly, I think it is because he is wearing a hat with an obnoxiously tall plume on it, and he's afraid the damned thing might fall off if he moves too fast."

Eleanor giggled. "Oh, that is part of his outfit, being Lord Warden," explained Eleanor.

"Did my father return from Scotland for the weddin'?" asked Lark.

"Nay, he's not down there," said Robin with a shrug.

"Oh, Lark, I'm so sorry," said Eleanor. "In all the excitement, I forgot to tell you that a missive arrived from Scotland this morning."

"Was it from my father?" asked Lark.

"Yes. He said he's sorry but they had already planned a huge celebration for your sister Heather's sixteenth birthday, so they won't be able to make it. They wished you had given them more notice. Your great-grandfather closed down the entire Horn and Hoof Tavern for the night, just to use it for the celebration. Uncle Storm said he needed to be there to guard the family from any danger."

"The only danger is of my Da drinkin' too much Mountain Magic," said Lark, speaking of the potent whisky her great grandfather brewed. "I want to be here for yer weddin' but I also miss my family. I wish I could join them."

"Me too," said Florie. "I miss Scotland, Mother."

"Well, convince that scribe of a husband of yours you want to go back for the celebration, and I'll get you there by tomorrow so you can join your family," offered Robin.

"Really?" asked Lark. "I would like that. That way, I can be here for Eleanor's weddin' and also be with Heather to celebrate her birthday."

"Lark, you know if you leave, we'll miss you," said Eleanor.

"Then we'll be back for Christmas," said Lark. "Dustin and I agreed to live sometimes in England and other times in Scotland, so we can spend time with everyone."

"Aye, come back for Christmas. Everyone can join me at my castle for the holiday," said Robin. "I plan on having a huge celebration."

"I'd like that," said Lark.

"We all would," said Raven. "However, those plans will need to wait. Right now, our husbands and Eleanor's husband-to-be are all patiently waiting for us in the great hall. I'll bet

Connor is even more nervous than anyone, waiting for the wedding to begin."

"That's right. We have a wedding to go to, and I say, let's go have some fun," said Rose, leading the way to the door.

Raven picked up the hem of the long train of Eleanor's gown, and Lark picked up the bridal bouquet of flowers. Then they all headed to the great hall for Eleanor and Connor's very special day.

CONNOR STILL HAD a hard time believing this was all real. Just a week ago he was doomed to be the hangman for the rest of his life, after the death of his father. Now, he was a noble again, a squire, and about to be married to the most beautiful girl alive. This was a dream come true. He started feeling like mayhap he did believe in God and angels, and heaven and hell after all.

Now, instead of living a life of hell, he would feel as if he were in heaven every day of his life.

"Brother, are you ready?" asked Leoric, dressed like a noble, coming to Connor's side. "I have the rings right here." He held up the rings on his finger and smiled.

"Leoric, you seem so happy," said Connor. "I think this life of a noble will suit you just fine."

"I'm glad you're going to be a knight someday, Connor. You deserve it."

"Well, so do you," said Connor. "Someday you'll be a knight as well, and then later—much later—so will Alaric."

Connor's gaze flashed over to little Alaric and Ginevra who were sitting with Eleanor's mother, Lady Echo. The woman had already accepted them into their family. Eleanor's father, Garrett, had offered to let all of Connor's siblings come to

Hythe and stay at his castle where they would be fostered by him.

"Nay, I will never be a knight," said Leoric.

"Don't be silly. Of course you will," said Connor. "And with the Lord Warden mentoring you, I guarantee that in time you will even get over being so squeamish. After all, he was my mentor once, and is a good man."

"I'm sure he is, Connor, but I've decided I don't want to be a knight," explained Leoric.

"No? Why not? What else would you do?"

"After everything that has happened, I've had some time to think. Connor, I've decided to join the Order."

"What?" Connor's eyes sprang open wide. "You are going to be a monk? Are you sure?"

"Yes, I am more than sure. I feel it is my calling. I don't ever want to kill anyone or assist in cleaning up dead bodies ever again."

"Leoric, you just need time to get over what we've been through. I'm sure that after a while you'll change your mind and want to be a knight too."

"Nay, I won't, Connor. When we stayed at the abbey, I saw the peaceful lifestyle of the monks and nuns and it felt right. That is what I want to do. Forever."

"Well, if that is your decision, then so be it," said Connor, putting his hand on Leoric's shoulder. "I will support you with whatever you decide to do, because you are my brother. And I love you," added Connor, almost afraid to say it aloud. After almost losing Leoric, he thought it was important to tell his brother what he meant to him. Connor had gone too many years thinking he'd never love anyone again, and actually it felt good to say it. Telling Eleanor he loved her was one thing. Telling one's family members was another. Connor's father had never said he loved his children, and Connor hoped to start a new tradition right now. His children, when he had them someday, would always know that their father loved them.

"Thank you, Connor. That means the world to me. I love you, too," said his brother. "However, I don't think Father would have agreed with my decision to join the Order. I am sure he is probably rolling over in his grave right now, just knowing that I am going to be a monk instead of a warrior like him."

"Well, I'm sure Mother would have given you her blessing, so I think it all evens out," Connor told him. They both had a good laugh about that.

Music started up from the gallery overhead. The musicians played flutes and lyres and even a hurdy-gurdy, taking everyone's attention, letting them know that the wedding was about to begin.

When Connor looked over to the entrance of the great hall, he froze. The Lord Warden walked down the aisle slowly, with Eleanor holding on to his arm. Raven followed behind, straightening Eleanor's long train. Lark walked along the aisles, watching as her daughter Florie threw rose petals on the path where Eleanor would step.

The hall was crowded with the families of each of them, and the nobles were all sitting up front. The dais was set for the wedding feast that would take place right after they said their vows.

Connor couldn't stop looking at Eleanor as she walked up the aisle with her father to join him. She seemed to like wearing green, and it complemented her vibrant red hair. This gown looked exquisite. The long, emerald-green gown was made of velvet, with long white tippets, sleeves that fell well past her hands and touched the ground. A long cape made of a sheer fabric was lined with bright gold lace. The bodice was also covered in gold lace with a high neckline. Her hair was plaited, and interwoven with tiny white flowers. Her head was covered by a small veil attached to a gold circlet headpiece.

Eleanor held an autumn bouquet of yellow, white, and crimson wildflowers tied together by a trailing long, colorful conglomeration of satin ribbons.

"God's eyes, she is beautiful," he mumbled under his breath, as her father stopped and handed her over to Connor. Connor held out his arm and Eleanor took it. They both turned and stood in front of the priest.

The wedding was short and simple, and that is exactly what Connor preferred. All he wanted was to hear the words *I do*, making Eleanor his wife. He couldn't wait to consummate the marriage. Tonight, he would sleep soundly for the first time since becoming son to a hangman. Tonight, he would have sweet dreams, holding Eleanor in his arms as they made love and their bodies melded into one.

They repeated their vows and he heard Eleanor say those magical words, *I do*.

Then they exchanged rings, completing the ceremony, as the priest pronounced them man and wife.

"You may kiss the bride," said Father Francis, the same priest who had married Connor's parents so very long ago.

Connor turned to Eleanor, slowly lifting her veil, pushing it to the back of her head. Her clear, hazel eyes held so much love that Connor swore he could feel it engulfing him and flowing through his entire body.

"I love you, Eleanor," he said, leaning in and gently kissing her on the mouth, right in front of everyone.

"I love you, too, Connor," she said, smiling from ear to ear.

The crowd cheered and clapped, and then the nobles came forward to congratulate them on their marriage.

"Connor, I'm not sure if you remember my brothers, Ethan and Edgar," said Eleanor, introducing them to him.

"Aye, of course I do," he said, shaking their hands. While Ethan was about the same age as Eleanor, Edgar was older, and really the son of the Lord Warden's dead brother.

"Welcome back to being a noble," said Ethan. He was a good-looking man and a charmer when it came to the ladies. Or at least, that is what Connor heard from Eleanor.

"Eleanor, I didn't think you'd ever get married," said Edgar, who was a few years older than she. "Or that you'd get married before Ethan, anyway."

"Me?" asked Ethan, his hand thumping against his chest. "Edgar, you're older than both of us. I think it's your turn next."

"Well, mayhap we should both go observe the single ladies here today," said Edgar, walking away with Ethan.

The abbess, Sister Sybil, and Sister Barbara were the next to congratulate them.

"We are going to miss you at the abbey," said Sister Barbara, taking Eleanor's hands in hers.

"Aye," agreed Sister Sybil. "Who is going to watch over those little girls?"

"Oh, you won't have to worry about that," Eleanor told them. "Tom and Alice from town are going to take them."

"The butcher?" asked Sister Barbara.

"Yes," said Eleanor.

"Is that good?" asked the abbess. "I mean, they couldn't seem to handle that boy who is a thief and was almost hanged."

"Oh, don't worry about Finnian," Connor told the nuns. "I can promise you that after his close brush with death, he'll never steal again."

"That's right," said Eleanor. "He has already changed and

is getting along nicely with Tom and Alice. Finnian is going to learn the business from Tom. He also promised to help watch over little Lena and Margaret. Alice is happy all the time now, and loves having so many children. They'll be visiting Edna and Albert at the farm regularly, so the girls can spend time with Bertram and Hamlin, and to play with the dog."

"Do you mean those serfs?" asked Sister Barbara.

"Yes, but they are not serfs anymore," said Eleanor, looking over and smiling at Connor. "You see, Connor and I bought their freedom. Now, Edna and Albert are no longer tied to the land or to the new lord of Marvane Castle, whoever that might be."

"That was so thoughtful of you, Lady Eleanor," said the nuns, congratulating her once more and then leaving to mingle with the crowd.

"Eleanor," said Robin, walking up with Lark and Florie. "I am sorry my sisters and parents aren't here, but they couldn't make it here on such short notice."

"I understand," said Eleanor. "This wasn't a normal wedding. We never even posted the wedding banns."

"The good news is that my family will all be visiting at my new castle in Shrewsbury for Christmas. I invited all the cousins and aunts and uncles. It is going to be a huge celebration."

"I can't wait to see it," Eleanor told him.

"I just wanted to tell you that I'll be escorting Lark and Florie to Scotland, first thing in the morning."

"Aye, we're goin' to the Horn and Hoof in Glasgow for my sister Heather's birthday celebration," said Lark.

"It'll take a good two days at least to get there," said Connor. "Won't you miss the celebration by the time you arrive?"

"I dinna think so," said Lark, giggling, resting her hands on her daughter's shoulders. "The last celebration my great-grandda had at his tavern lasted for an entire week."

"Yes, the MacKeefes are known for their long and bountiful celebrations," said Eleanor.

"And their whisky," added Robin with a laugh. "Don't forget about that potent Mountain Magic."

They said their goodbyes, and Raven and Rose walked up next.

"Congratulations to both of you. I am so happy for the way things turned out," Raven said, giving them both a hug.

"Aye," said Rose, hugging them as well. "You make a perfect couple. And the best part is that Connor has his life back again."

"Nay, the best part is having Eleanor for my wife," said Connor, kissing her and putting his arm around her.

"Where are your husbands?" asked Eleanor, scanning the room.

"Jonathon is showing Rook some new thing he got for the forge," said Raven, shaking her head. "He just couldn't wait, he was so excited about it."

"Aye, and even Lark's husband, Dustin, went with them," said Rose.

"Couldn't that have waited until later?" asked Eleanor.

Raven shook her head and rolled her eyes. "My brother seems to think he needs to know everything that goes on at Blake Castle, even though he doesn't live here anymore. I'm sure it was he who decided they needed to go to the forge at this very moment."

"Rook doesn't like change," Rose told them. "But since I keep changing things up at Rookrose Manor, he'll need to get used to it sooner or later."

"Everyone, please take a seat," Lord Corbett called out,

standing atop the dais with a goblet in his hand. "The Lord Warden would like to make a toast."

Once Eleanor and Connor were up at their seats, Eleanor's father raised his goblet in the air, standing up for all to see.

"I'd like to say I am elated that my daughter Eleanor has married Lord Connor Wyland," he called out loudly so all could hear.

Connor saw Rook, Dustin, and Jonathon hurry into the great hall and quickly take their seats at the dais.

Connor leaned over and whispered to Eleanor. "I'm not used to being called Lord Connor anymore."

"Well, that was your title before, and it is again, so get used to it," she whispered back.

"Now, I'd like to ask Lord Connor and Lady Eleanor to stand and say a word or two as well." Garrett looked over at then and nodded.

The crowd clapped as Garrett sat back down.

"What are we supposed to say?" Connor asked Eleanor.

"Just say what we feel about each other, I guess." She took his hand and they both stood up.

"You go first," she told him, as Connor picked up a goblet of wine and handed it to her and then picked up one for himself.

"All right," he said, clearing his throat and holding his goblet high in the air. "To my wife, Lady Eleanor. The most beautiful woman in the world. You have made all my dreams come true. All I can say is, I am so happy that you can forget my past and look forward to our future together. That you can accept me for who I am."

The crowd cheered and clapped and took a drink. Then it was Eleanor's turn.

"To my husband, Lord Connor," she said, smiling at him and raising her goblet high in the air. "Your past doesn't matter to me, because when I am with you, my heart soars. The happiness that fills me from being your wife encompasses me with every breath I take. And that love I feel, dear Husband, changes everything that was bad, to good. It truly elates me and excites me and makes me feel so lucky to be able to spend the rest of my life with you. Yes, Connor, I am so happy. Being with you makes me feel—in the best way ever—like I am truly ***Dancing on Air***."

FROM THE AUTHOR

I hope you enjoyed Eleanor and Connor's story and will take a moment to leave a review.

As I said at the beginning of this book, I stumbled upon the information in my research that a nobleman about to be executed could beg for mercy and accept the position of being the hangman in exchange for his life.

I had never heard this before and found it fascinating. When one's life is threatened, they are willing to do whatever it takes to be spared. The nobleman would lose his title, wealth, and any respect by taking the position, but at least he wouldn't lose his life.

As you see by what happened to Connor, sometimes a bad situation can turn even worse. I don't know how anyone could do the job of being an executioner, being shunned and avoided and hated by all. Of course, I couldn't bear to see Connor have to kill someone, so I worked around that and stopped that from happening before it was too late. I can't say any noble who was a hangman ever had their position reversed, but then again, this is my story and I like happy endings. I decided it could be no other way.

If you haven't already read about Raven, Rook, and Lark, please be sure to do so. Their stories are **Picking up the Gauntlet**, **A Rose Among Thorns**, and **Love Letters for Lady Lark**.

In my **Below the Salt Series**, I push the envelope, as I am known to do quite often. Nobles had to marry someone of their own status. They usually married for alliances, and hardly ever for love. In my *Below the Salt* Series, I pair up nobles with commoners.

Nobles sat upon a raised dais to eat. Salt was expensive, and the nobles had salt cellars filled on their table. Commoners, servants, and others were not so lucky to get much salt, or sometimes not even any at all. They sat at long trestle tables on benches instead of padded chairs. They ate brown bread, while the nobles had white.

The commoners sat lower with simple food to eat. The nobles were forbidden to marry anyone from Below the Salt.

Eleanor's cousin, Robin's story is next. You'll find out all about him in **Winter Sage**.

If you'd like to read Eleanor's parents' story, you can do so in *Lady in the Mist*, Book 5 of my Legacy of the Blade Series.

The Below the Salt Series follows the generations of the Blake family. If you'd like to read about Corbett Blake and his wife Devon, you can find their story in **Lord of the Blade**, Book 1 of my **Legacy of the Blade Series**. Be sure to read the **Legacy of the Blade Prequel**, to find out what makes Lord Corbett Blake such a hardened man. The stories of his long-lost siblings can be found in **Lady Renegade**, **Lord of Illusion**, and **Lady of the Mist**. Orrick, the sorcerer from the *Legacy of the Blade* Series has his crazy story told in the last book, and one of my favorites, called **Keeper of the Flame**.

Stop by and visit my **Website**. You can follow me on **Amazon**, **Bookbub**, **Goodreads**, **Facebook,** and **Twitter**. I also have a **Private Readers' Group** on Facebook that I invite you to join.

If you would like to stay informed of my new books and also sales, please be sure to subscribe to my **newsletter**.

Thank you,

Elizabeth Rose

ABOUT ELIZABETH

Elizabeth Rose is an award-winning, bestselling author of over 100 books and counting. She writes medieval, historical, contemporary, paranormal, and western romance. Her books are available as EBooks, paperbacks, and some audiobooks as well.

Her favorite characters in her works include dark, dangerous and tortured heroes, and feisty, independent heroines who know how to wield a sword. She loves writing 14th century medieval novels, and is well-known for her many series.

Elizabeth loves the outdoors. In the summertime, you can find her in her secret garden with her laptop, swinging in her hammock working on her next book. Elizabeth is a born storyteller and passionate about sharing her works with her readers.

Please be sure to visit her website at **Elizabethrosenovels.com** to read excerpts from any of her novels and get sneak peeks at covers of upcoming books. You can follow her on **Twitter, Facebook, Goodreads** or **BookBub.** Be sure to sign up for her **newsletter** so you don't miss out on new releases or upcoming events.

Click to join **Elizabeth Rose's Readers' Group.**

ALSO BY ELIZABETH ROSE

Medieval Series:

Legendary Bastards of the Crown Series

Seasons of Fortitude Series

Secrets of the Heart Series

Legacy of the Blade Series

Daughters of the Dagger Series

MadMan MacKeefe Series

Barons of the Cinque Ports Series

Holiday Knights Series

Highland Chronicles Series

Pirate Lords Series

Highland Outcasts

Medieval/Paranormal Series:

Elemental Magick Series

Greek Myth Fantasy Series

Tangled Tales Series

Portals of Destiny

Contemporary Series:

Tarnished Saints Series

Working Man Series

Western Series:

Cowboys of the Old West Series

And More!

Please visit http://elizabethrosenovels.com